Silkscreen

Caroline Pitcher

Also by Caroline Pitcher

Mine

11 o'Clock Chocolate Cake

For younger readers

Ghost in the Glass

Silkscreen

Caroline Pitcher

EGMONT

For Richard, who makes everything possible

When illness changed my eyesight, it set me thinking
about the way we look at things. Sometimes it's
easier to turn away.

Thanks to the Arts Council for giving *Silkscreen*
a Writers' Award for work in progress.

Visit Caroline Pitcher's web site:
www.carolinepitcher.co.uk

First published in Great Britain in 2000 by Mammoth
Reissued 2002 by Egmont Books Limited
239 Kensington High Street, London W8 6SA

ISBN 1 4052 0275 0

10 9 8 7 6 5 4 3 2 1

A CIP catalogue record for this title is available from the British Library

Typeset by Avon DataSet Ltd, Bidford on Avon, B50 4JH
Printed in Great Britain by Cox & Wyman Ltd, Reading, Berkshire

Contents

PART ONE

A gathering of shadows

ABOVE DARK WATER STANDS A MILL.

IN THE WINDOW BURNS A CANDLE.

BY ITS LIGHT YOU SEE A FACE.

DON'T TURN AWAY.

ONE

Toastie Queen

Last October half-term, I spent most of my time with a toasted sandwich maker.

'Why can't you wash the thing up when you've used it?' said my brother Sam.

'Because *I* did the cooking. *I* don't wash up. Not in this house.'

Sam rolled his eyes to heaven. 'It wasn't a banquet, Rachel. It was only a cheese toastie.'

'*Four* cheese toasties if you don't mind.'

'Ye-es, and three of them were yours. You and your friends'. And what a mess you made!' He plunged his hands into the sink and the sandwich maker's insides surfaced from the bubbles like a submarine.

'It's stuck all over,' grumbled Sam. 'No wonder. You cut bread like breeze blocks. You put too much filling in. Your sandwiches don't *seal*, Rachel. Your sandwiches *leak*.'

'Oh the *shame*!' I sneered. You'd think I had hair sprouting out of my nose.

There was a whimper. Our dog Wally pushed his nose into my hand. He turned big eyes from me to Sam and back again. He hated it when we argued, so I patted the pointy bit on top of his head to reassure him that his world wasn't falling apart.

Sam hadn't finished. 'Cheese and pickle doesn't come off if you leave it to set rock hard.'

'The blurb says the sandwich maker is non-stick. It's not *my* fault if that's a lie,' I said, flicking a bubble from Wally's back.

My friends burst into the kitchen.

'Ooooh, Sam, just in time!' cried Nikki, waving a glass at him. 'Please will you wash this up for me?' She snatched a plate from Gemma, who was sheltering behind her. 'And this?' she cried. 'We knew you were here, Sam, 'cos of Wally. I said, wherever Sam is, Wally won't be far away.'

Wally's ears pricked at his name. They were tufty ears and would have looked better on a guinea-pig than on a big black dog. I thought, it's not just Wally who hangs around Sam.

My brother said, 'Of course I'll wash them up. I like my glasses sparkly clean. Are there any more up in Rachel's hovel? It's like a shantytown up there.'

My brother is just so normal and orderly.

You should see *his* room! A nightmare of neatness, with little robot filing cabinets, pots of pens (ballpoints in one, a few fountain pens in another, highlighting pens in a third) and even a pot of plain wood lead pencils, all sharpened to silver quills. There are shirts on hangers all facing the same way as if they are on a bus, folders carefully filed, shelves of books in alphabetical order, a vast cage of combed chinchillas clean and odour-free. All that floor-space wasted.

'Go and get the glasses, Gemma,' ordered Nikki, pushing her away.

'Rachel's not much good at glasses,' confided my brother. 'They come out more smeary than they went in. And her toasted sandwiches are in a class on their own. She's Toastie Queen, aren't you, Rache?'

He turned to me with a wide and wicked grin. I stuck my tongue out.

Sam drives me mad. He is so obvious. What you see is what you get with him. He's like Dad, no hidden depths or surprise moves, no secret ways. I can read him like a baby's book. I know what he'll do and say next, and it's usually something to wind me up, especially in front of my friends.

Sam is clever in a flat sort of way. That term he was studying for A levels, four of them, all hard science and biology stuff. He's always wanted to do something medical. A brain surgeon? A vet? He's always been good with animals. Wally adores him. Sam is the leader of his pack,

4

more than anyone else in the family. It was Sam who trained the rabbit to use a cat litter tray, Sam who pushed pills down the cat's throat with a pencil, past the pointed stalactite teeth.

My brother has always been close to slimy things. I've been brought up with snakes down the sofa, lizards basking in lamplight, a toad almost roasted in the oven. You get used to it. We had buckets full of frogspawn. We had fat newts squirming in an old tin bath.

The only thing Sam didn't keep were birds. 'They should be free to fly,' he said.

For all these creatures, Sam was boss. They never bit him.

No. They bit me, especially Hannibal, that murderous golden hamster.

When I was little I bit back. I bit Sam. That's what he says, anyway.

My brother was born in long trousers. He's always been an apprentice adult. Sometimes that's useful. When I was about eight I didn't want to go to school because a girl called Lisa got her friends to chase me round the playground and call me names. So Sam took himself off up the road to see her mother. That's right, her *mother*.

I think all the adults were surprised, but I tell you what, the bullying stopped.

Gemma slouched in with a leaning tower of mugs and

glasses for Sam to wash and Nikki arranged herself by the cooker to watch. Sam didn't mind at all. Every now and then he glanced at them and smiled.

'Will you and Adam be doing rugby this term?' asked Nikki.

'Yes, we'll be doing rugby,' he said, drying his hands. 'Now, if you'll excuse me, my biology notes are waiting. I'm leaving the sandwich thing to soak.' Pointed glance at me. He disappeared upstairs and we heard Wally clicking after him.

I turned to Nikki to talk about going to the cinema, and stopped. A smile was playing around Nikki's lips and there was a faraway look in her eyes. It was a faraway-down-the-rugby-field sort of look. I knew that she and Gemma and others hung around the nets watching the boys from the sixth form practise.

I went with them once. What a yawn. Lots of mud and grunting. I couldn't be bothered after that. My brother's friends are just so close. So safe. I seem to have known them all my life. There's nothing reckless, nothing exotic, somehow . . . nothing mad, bad or dangerous to know. Same clothes, same music, same haircuts, same jokes. They're all right, I suppose, especially his friend Adam, he's good for lifts. He's bumbly. The only mad thing about Adam is his choice in toasties – Brie with peach and sultana chutney. That's a messy one, I can tell you.

'Suppose we'd better be going,' said Nikki. Now Sam has disappeared upstairs, I thought. It's strange to think people fancy your brother. It seems almost unnatural.

'I'll ring you about the cinema,' I said. 'Maybe we could go on Thursday afternoon? I thought I'd ask Helen too.'

That stopped them in their tracks. They stared at each other, words in their eyes but not on their lips.

'Helen?' breathed Nikki. 'You mean, Helen Anderson?'

'Yes. Helen. Helen Anderson.'

Their eyes were still locked together. They wrinkled their noses.

'She's so uncool,' said Nikki. 'That haircut! Orang-utans have hair like that. Her mother cuts it. And what about her voice, Rachel!' Nikki put on a crazy accent: 'Gizz yer boo-ook, will yer. Ah went t'ut doctor's and missed me maffs so ah've got ter catch OOOOP!'

Nikki and Gemma capsized, clutching their stomachs. Some of the laughter was put on. Then their eyes met and they began real laughing.

And then I had to laugh too. Nikki was so funny doing that voice.

At last we slowed down. 'I quite like her,' I said.

'Who?'

'Helen. Helen Anderson. I like talking to her.'

'Oh.' Nikki shrugged her thin shoulders and said, 'Are you sure about that, Rachel?'

'Yes.' I was just about to add, she's different, when I saw the signs: DANGER!

Nikki and Gemma left and I turned my attention to the sandwich maker. It sat there, white and gleaming, a clean, neat, magic machine. The outside was clean, anyway. It was a present to the family from Mum. I suppose she thought it would save her time. We could cook snacks. I suppose she hoped we'd wash it all up again. And we did. Sometimes.

I decided to try a chocolate-spread toastie. I lifted the machine's insides from the washing-up bowl. The cheese had gone all stretchy and could be peeled away, like old nail varnish. Very satisfying. Sam had missed a treat there.

I patted its insides dry and prepared the sandwich. It was a bit thick but I forced the machine shut with a satisfying *snap*, like a little handbag. It sat there sizzling busily, making my sandwich.

I wondered who would wash it up when Sam went off to college?

That October was when it all began.

2
Empress of the shopping arcade

On the Friday it was my mother's birthday.

'How many years now, Mum?' said Sam, big-eyed, feigning ignorance.

'Forty-six,' she murmured, head down.

Dad got the afternoon off work for once. I couldn't remember him doing that before. He always worked steady hours, in shift patterns, not like other fathers who seemed to take time off whenever they felt like it.

So we all went out together, Mum, Dad, Sam and I, for presents and a meal.

I hated it when I had to ride in the back of the car with Sam. We were the little children, they were the power people in front. Dad was driving. He always drove when they were together. I stared at the two heads, Mum's set a little lower down than Dad's. Dad's head moved to check a junction. He should have shaved. He looked as if he had poppy seeds sprinkled over his chin. He's too old for stubble to look good.

After a while she asked, 'Where are we going, love?' He didn't answer. He spun the wheel and roared down a little lane.

'Burn rubber, Dad!' I shouted.

He braked suddenly. Mum ricocheted in her seat and cried, 'Stop it, Mike! Don't!'

A sea of white heads was surging up the lane towards the car. It was an old ladies' coach trip. I'd seen crinkly crowds here before. They went to the rather expensive factory shop for cardigans and two-pieces. They had even brought a couple of token old gents with newspapers clamped in their armpits.

Dad sat there, muttering. His foot squeezed the accelerator. Sam leaned forward and hissed, 'Go on, Dad! See how many you can get at one go!'

Sometimes I think men are horrible.

The car was surrounded. The old ladies bobbed and smiled. I had a fantasy of them dragging my father from the car and bearing him aloft, the sacrificial middle-aged man, back to their sheltered housing, and then . . .

'Stop sniggering, Rachel,' he snapped. 'Be patient for once. Your mother wants to go to the factory shop to choose her birthday present.'

'No I don't,' said Mum.

'Eh? I thought this was the best place. I thought you always went here?'

'I do,' she said. 'And so I want to go into town, to a *different* shop.'

I noticed that my mother had quite a lot of make up on, for her. Brown mascara and a rosy lipstick, even some colour on her cheeks. She hadn't put it on very well. I leaned forward and tried to blend it in with my fingertips.

My father frowned. A different shop? He checked in his mirrors for old women, then turned the car round and headed into town.

We split up in the shopping centre. 'Enjoy yourselves, girls. Don't spend too much,' said my father as he headed for a PC Palace with Sam.

Mum and I didn't often shop together. It could be hard work, because we argued about what she would and wouldn't buy me. Today it was for her. I'd better make sure she didn't buy a really short skirt or witch's shoes, not that she ever had done before, but today she was in a strange sort of birthday mood, excited and out of reach.

We loitered before dress-shop windows. 'Let's look here,' said Mum by a department store.

My heart sank. We wandered through ranks of dingy dresses in limp acrylic, navy, mushroom, turnip. Who wore these things? Not *my* mother.

'Come on, Rachel,' she said, spinning on her heel.

I followed her along an arcade and into a shop like Aladdin's cave. They were playing old music with harps and tinkly guitars and waily voices, the sort of music Mum and Dad like. 'They're not exactly clothes to do your gardening in, Mum,' I said, looking at the swathes of silk, satin, velvet and net, the beads and sequins spangling in pools of soft light.

I could see why the women liked these clothes, even though they were expensive. They were too much for me, too fairytale and romantic. They were clothes to wear when falling off the *Titanic*.

The shop was busy with women my mother's age and younger, working their way methodically through the racks. Shopping was a serious business here. Isn't it anywhere? I was just surprised to see all these mothers so fixed on clothes.

We'd be here a while. I saw strings of beads and satin bags barely big enough to keep your gum in. I found some sweet little earrings, blue crescent moons. I knew my mum; if I played it right she'd buy them for me.

Scarves and shawls hung in swathes, looking like the tent of some rich nomad prince. The colours rippled across the silk, spilling with each other as if the inks were still wet. I found a scarf of watercolour blue, green and gold, and let it slip through my hands again and again.

'It'd be like wearing one of those Monet lilyponds round your neck,' I mused.

'Oh really, Rachel!' she said. 'Oh!'

I turned round in time to see her heading for a rail of coats. Carefully, she took one down. It was deep, deep blue. She stood in front of a mirror with the coat held up before her. I sighed and followed.

The coat was long, down to her calves. It had a strange collar, a soft velvet cowl, sort of Empress out of *Star Wars* meets the Snow Queen. It was fitted to the waist. I saw with surprise that my mother had a waist left.

'It's a midnight coat,' she whispered. Her eyes were far away in some dream land.

It was an unusual colour, I had to admit. It was so dark you couldn't decide if the velvet was blue or black or violet. She would stand out in it. Everyone would look at her in that coat. It was like fancy dress. It was a fairytale coat.

She stroked the velvet thoughtfully. Then she twisted her neck round in the soft high collar to try to see the label. I scrabbled at the back of her neck to pull it out but in the end she had to take off the coat to see the price tag.

She froze. The fantasy was over.

'We couldn't possibly pay that!' she said. 'Not for a coat. Not for me.'

'There might be a cheap one, shop-soiled or ripped or something,' I said, rummaging through a rail marked SALE.

There wasn't. The coat was one on its own.

'Oh well. I don't know when I'd wear it anyway. It's not for me,' she said. 'I'll get something useful.'

Reluctantly she hung the coat up again.

I found a cool white top and went to try it on.

When I came out of the fitting-rooms, I couldn't see her. She must have gone, I thought, and went towards the door.

There was a woman sitting on a chair with her back to me, head listing towards her shoulder. Too old for Mum, I thought.

I walked round to the front of the chair.

'Mum?' I said.

She opened her eyes. For a second I don't think she knew where she was.

'I couldn't find you, Mum!' I said.

'Sorry, love,' she said. 'I'm tired and – er – I've got bit of a headache.' She smiled at me. 'I found some smart trousers. And a skirt. More me. Ah. Here they come!'

And there they were all right, just coming into the shop. Sam and Dad. My father. I wished he wasn't. The minute he saw us looking at him he started doing that stupid leaping (the shop music was dance now, not floaty old time). It was just like he always did, arms flailing like the sails of a windmill, the shop light shining on his bald patch. Why did he have those terrible baggy old jeans? He stepped and twizzled, a fraction of a beat behind the music, and Sam walked with him, grinning. He didn't mind.

A couple of women going out looked up to the ceiling to see what this clown was pointing at. I could have told them it was his *Grease* routine. I stepped behind a pillar. It was so embarrassing. Somewhere in his mind Dad knew his dancing was ridiculous, but somewhere else he dreamed he was a fit young dude again. If he ever was.

'Am I paying for your stuff too, Rachel?' he called a minute later. 'I can't believe you need any *more* clothes.'

'Mum said I could have it,' I retorted. '*And* these earrings too.'

He sighed heavily. 'So I'm paying for trousers and a skirt for your mother, and these things for you. Oh well. I'd better get the plastic out.'

I took his elbow and whispered, 'You got off lightly. She's bought that boring tailored stuff but what she really fancies is that Empress of Midnight coat. There. That velvet one.'

He grabbed the price label and turned it over. 'You must be joking.'

3
End of the day

It was that funny time of day when people disappear from the centre of the city. They stream on to buses and queue to get out of carparks and then just vanish into some suburbia. The shadows gather. In a way I like that time of day; it makes me think of cake and evenings with my family in front of a blazing fire.

There's no fire in the city. The shops shut. The assistants are desperate for you to leave so they can go home. Through the glass doors you see shadowless places with racks of clothes as if bodies had just stepped out of them and vanished into thin air.

'Nowhere for a decent cuppa now,' said Mum. 'Antonio's shuts at five thirty.' If we went shopping in the morning we used to go to an Italian place where the oldies' coffee was good and strong. I had foamy cappuccino thoroughly sprinkled with chocolate, and truly sticky lemon cake.

And sometimes their son was working there.

'Shall we go to a pub?' said Dad hopefully. But we'd have to sit inside and Mum hated the smoke. We wandered through the empty city centre, peering into restaurants. None of them was quite open yet.

'Sure you don't want to go home first, love?' asked Dad.

'Quite sure,' she said. 'It will get too late if we do that.'

Now, Mum's idea of lateness and mine were very different. But I was starving! So I said, 'Come on, Birthday Woman. Let's see if they're ready for us.' Because I knew she wanted to go for a Thai. She always did if we went out for a treat.

The lights shone on tables set with pale pink linen and the white vases with fresh carnations. I loved the wall-hanging of plump silver elephants, princes and flowers.

We were the first customers, of course. The manageress was sitting at a table with a pile of papers in front of her, doing her accounts. She stood up in surprise when we walked in, but smiled as she recognised us and beckoned us to a table. Then she went to turn on some suitably Thai-type music.

I saw Sam sniffing at the scents from the kitchen, lime and coconut, lemon-grass and coriander. Mmmm! He has been known to ask for egg and chips in a Balti house. He's so conservative. He went through a phase of refusing anything with garlic or chillies, and only wearing grey. And he always wears socks that match, and he cleans his shoes and doesn't leave them for Dad to do. That evening, he wore a sort of silky blue shirt, not bad, but he still looked too smart.

The only time I've seen Sam truly messy was when he had trifle all over his face. And I mean all over. You see, we were bickering one meal time. Dad wasn't there and poor old Mum kept wittering, 'Stop it, you two!' and then Sam called me fat and I just couldn't resist it – I lobbed trifle at him. I must have done four or five spoonfuls, then I stopped to revel in that brief, marvellous moment of triumph at the horror on his face and the custard on his nose, sponge and raspberries trickling down his cheeks. Wow! It was worth the beating-up that followed, and Mum wailing, 'My trifle! Stop it, you two. What about your father? It's his favourite and it's all over Sam!'

Tonight she said, 'You're not having chips, Sam. Not on my birthday.'

'As if I would!' he cried, affronted.

He ate everything that night, cashew nuts and noodles, satay sauce, and that was not typical. I can't cope with an unpredictable brother.

It was a feast, that meal, a feast for the senses. The little fritters that arrived for starters were adorned with birds and flowers so thin they looked as if they were cut from orange and white paper, but they were sculpted out of vegetables. Sam picked up a carrot pelican and pretended to bite its head off and my parents laughed. It was a moment to keep. I've thought of it often.

'They'll complain about the garlic,' I said, in a little space between the mouthfuls.

'Who will?' asked Mum.

'Nikki and Gemma. They're coming over tomorrow.'

'What about that Helen girl? Couldn't she go to the cinema with you all yesterday?'

'Oh. By the time I got round to ringing her, it was too late. She was out.'

I felt my face go pink.

I wished Mum wouldn't look at me like that.

'But you like her, don't you, Rachel?'

'Yes.'

'And Gemma and Nikki don't, I suppose.'

'No. Well, they don't think she's cool. She's different from us.'

'Is she different from you?'

'A bit. She doesn't really fit with our little lot.'

'But you like her?'

'Yes.'

'Trust yourself, Rachel.'

She was always saying that, always on about, think for yourself, Rachel, no such thing as a group. But there *were* groups, and I belonged to one, and I wanted to stay in it.

I said, 'They think Helen has no style.'

'What they mean is, she doesn't make them look good,' said my mother. How I hated it when she stuck her nose in like that.

She said, 'Don't worry too much about doing what the others want, darling.'

'I suppose that's your Thought for the Day,' I sneered. 'Mother's Moral.'

She shrugged. 'Yes,' she said. 'Be true to yourself. Follow your heart. Always.' She pushed her plate away and sank back in her chair.

'You haven't eaten much of your birthday feast, love,' said Dad, scooping more noodles on to his plate.

She put her hand over her eye as if she didn't want us to see it. I think her eyelid must have been flickering, you know, that twitching you get when you're tired. Sometimes Mum's eye looked a bit droopy and old.

I looked at the Thai woman in the yellow and gold dress. She was so elegant and shiny, and slim as a spring onion. I wondered if Mum was trying to diet. But she wasn't really fat, just sort of stretched.

I thought, next year Sam goes to college. He is sure to get in.

And so next year there will be just the three of us.

That October was the beginning of the story. I'd like to stay here, but I have to move on.

PART TWO

Down into darkness

THE RIVER RACES THROUGH THE SECRET DALE.
LOOK UP AT THE WINDOW WHERE THE CANDLELIGHT
FLICKERS.
THERE'S A FACE. CALLING OUT. ISN'T THERE?
DON'T TURN AWAY FROM IT.
IF YOU TURN BACK TO THE REST OF THE WORLD, THE LIGHT
WILL GO OUT.

4

It's Dad's fault

Hi Sam!

Bet you didn't expect a postcard so soon. This is where I'm staying. Narrow Dale Mill. It's run by complete freaks and it's haunted. Otherwise, it's just fine. Hope you're enjoying college. Bye now!

Your Little Sister Rachel

It's Dad's fault I'm here. Dad doesn't like me hanging around at home on my own. I'd be fine, but Dad doesn't understand that.

'You need something to do, Rachel,' he said. 'It'll be good for your history. And Beth from your year is going too. Why are you pulling that face?'

Because I don't want to be cooped up with anyone. Not at the moment. Beth's all right, I suppose, although she does go on about looking like a supermodel, and she changes her clothes ten times a day. I don't know her very well. She's not in my form. Lucky Beth. I've got Miss Benson. Miss Benson doesn't like me. She told Dad I was arrogant, that I wouldn't try to fit in.

Beth is lucky not to have Miss Benson. Beth is at the mill because her parents have gone off to Ibiza. They say Beth doesn't need Ibiza. They say she's already been to France and Spain with school.

I haven't. I haven't been anywhere nice.

Narrow Dale Mill in darkest Derbyshire is certainly *not* nice.

The mill brochure looks as if it's been given an electric shock. It's all shatter print and exclamation marks. It boasts about '*THE rich historical holiday experience! The old cotton mills come to life! A completely new venture for Narrow Dale Mill! A holiday to remember!*' It's certainly one I'll remember.

We happy holidaymakers had to meet in the middle of Bakewell. There were a dozen of us. It was a beautiful October day, blue sky and sharp sun. The trees were golden and red as if they were full of little fairy lights.

We stood waiting to make the last part of our journey.

It was by horse and cart. Yes, you did hear right.

I was glad I had my jeans on because we had to step high up into the cart and perch on a cold seat.

I liked the horse. He was huge and his iron-grey sides were dappled like a snowstorm. He put his great head down and pulled us along a track through the dale. The clop-clopping of his hooves was thrown back from the steep banks as if Indian braves crouched up there with tom-toms.

It was very bumpy, and we all screamed and shrieked as we went deeper into the narrow dale, down into darkness. It was like being swallowed down a gullet. I began to shiver. The sun had left us. We clopped round a bend and came upon a lake of black glass. Beyond it a building reared up as sheer as a cliff.

This must be Narrow Dale Mill. It looked more like Vampire Roost, a film set, one of those old cardboard frontier towns in Westerns. If only.

The mill is built of pale limestone. It has arched windows that make it look surprised. There are two blocks, with a high walkway between.

That first day I saw someone up on the walkway.

'Look!' I cried, but Beth didn't see it. Mind you, Beth is a bit dozy.

Perhaps it was a stone figure on the walkway? It was quite still, as if it was frozen. Perhaps it was a gargoyle, I said to myself. I don't think you get gargoyles on mills, although there is plenty of water for them to spew out. Wherever you are at Narrow Dale, you can hear water. You never get away from the sound of the river and the mill race, tumbling through the earth and the iron teeth of the sluice. The first time I heard the great water wheel begin to turn in its pit I was terrified.

I think of my brother Sam. I feel nicer about him when I'm not with him. I wish he was here to have a laugh with, because it's really the *hysterical* holiday experience, not the *historical* one. We have to dress up like mill apprentices of olde yesteryear. Honestly! I have a long homespun dress in a charming shade of brown, a white smock and a strange bonnet with flaps so that I look like a lop-eared bunny. Oh, and clogs. I forgot the clogs. Shiny clogs. We pretend to be poor child labour, but we're all so crispy clean and fragrant in our fabric-softened costumes and neatly ironed smocks, no real apprentice would be fooled for a second. Still, we've been promised days out. There's a theme park down the road. That'll be good. There's a picnic. We're going swimming one day, and shopping in Bakewell. There's table tennis and telly.

And then there's *him*.

The trouble is, I think he may be a ghost.

5

Ghost at the window

Salut Sam!
Porridge for breakfast. Salt to go with it. Great. But you
can have golden syrup too. Oatcakes and cheese for
lunch. It's local cheese called Hartington Stilton, or you
can have smelly old goat stuff. Disgusting.

Rachel

I am not going to tell my brother about the ghost. He won't
believe me. I've decided that I'm going to write to Sam
every day, to keep myself sane. I bought lots of postcards at
the desk in the entrance, but there's only the one picture,
of Narrow Dale Mill, naturally. I've got my precious little
pen with me, the gold one, the one with my initials on the
side. R.W.

I suppose I'd better tell you about Mr Silk.

Mr Silk is in charge here. He's called Mill Director in the

brochure, but we have to call him Master. Master of the Mill. Principal Loony.

He is *weird*!

Mr Silk brings round a party of visitors as we stand stiffly in our costumes. He is dressed up in a frock-coat that dazzles like a cut jewel. It makes me think of oil on water, that sheen of blue and pink and green so you never know what colour it really is.

He has long, sleek, chestnut-brown hair with a few wisps of silver at the side. It curls on his lace collar. A distinguished gentleman of the past, that's the impression. He is quite graceful for a middle-aged man, I suppose.

His nose is beaky. Sideways on he's like a hawk.

Mr Silk talks to the visitors. It is a cultured, pleasant, sing-song voice. There's just a hint of Derbyshire in it. Mr Silk goes on and on and on. The adults listen obediently. Their children squirm, eyes looking for an escape route. Mr Silk waves his thin hands as if he is conjuring rainbow scarves from his sleeves.

He says, 'You've all heard of King Cotton, ladies and gentlemen?'

Because you're going to now, whether you like it or not.

'King Cotton made the mill masters rich. Remember Sir Richard Arkwright in his glittering carriage?' *No.* 'Jedediah Strutt in Belper?' *No.*

Mr Silk puts his long hands softly together as if he's

praying. He says, 'Old Jedediah was a true philanthropist. In today's market-led society, Thornton's chocolates help to fund Belper schools. How *sweet* of them! Jedediah Strutt built a school for his mill workers with money from his mill. Bless his *little cotton socks*!'

Mr Silk pauses and looks round for laughter. The adults fall about. I don't.

He says, 'The mill masters gave orphans and paupers work, ladies and gentlemen. I think it is a twentieth-century fantasy, a fairytale, to talk of their cruelty to their child labour. In any case, the Factory Acts put a halt to the employment of children.'

What? I want to retort that in my history lessons it wasn't like that. The employment of children stopped because it became too expensive. You had to house and feed them. That was the only reason they let them go. But I'm polite and I know when to keep my mouth shut. (All right, Sam, I can hear your hollow laughter . . .)

Mr Silk says, 'Nowadays, ladies and gentlemen, we are surprised to think of children working. But there *are* child slaves in the world, making clothes and shoes, being used as prostitutes, even working as camel jockeys. Yes! Children are exploited in heathen lands. Not in *this* country, of course, ladies and gentlemen.'

How does he know for sure? Mr Smug! How can . . .

There's a movement in the corner of my eye.

Through the window I can see the brick bridge that

spans the courtyard high up between two buildings. There's a figure on it.

Mr Silk's voice drones on. 'Dear visitors, you may call me soft, you may even call me a twentieth-century philanthropist. I *love* the Bible, ladies and gentlemen! I love its poetry and its wisdom. I read it for sheer pleasure of mind, and my favourite text has always been, "*Suffer the little children to come unto me*." This year, for the first time, I am helping those less fortunate than ourselves.'

That brings me back to the here and now. Fast.

He leans forward to the visitors, as if he's telling them a secret that everyone can hear. He waves his hand and a long finger points towards us.

'Some of *these* young folk are disadvantaged, ladies and gentlemen. They are in need. They are the small, disadvantaged folk hiding in the cracks between the floorboards of modern-day life.'

'Aaah!' breathes the audience. Many put their heads on one side and smile. A man of compassion, they think.

'Yes,' he murmurs. 'They are children in need indeed.'

Does he think this is a prayer meeting?

'They are in need indeed,' he intones, eyes closed.

Why do I feel sick?

Because he means *me*.

I am one of today's disadvantaged. Dad had to stop work for months. Now he's got a new job, but for ages we were 'hard-up', 'stressed', 'a dysfunctional family' – all those buzz words. It's been difficult for all of us. I *thought* our doctor was extra nosey when I went about my skin. (It's been worse lately.) He kept asking if I felt 'stressed', 'confused', 'lethargic', 'insomniac'. You name the silly word, he said it. Maybe he had something to do with getting me on this so-called holiday on the cheap.

I don't want to hear Mr Silk congratulating himself.

And I don't live in the cracks between *anybody's* floor-boards. I live in Cedar Road! Mr Silk makes us sound like the Borrowers.

I turn away to hide my anger.

There's a face in the window. A good-looking face. It's Young, Dark and Male. His hair is quite long and soft, black, almost to his neck. He's scowling through the window at us, through the small panes. His eyes are smoky hollows. They meet mine and my heart flutters in my chest as if there's a bird caught in my ribcage.

He stares at me for a long moment. How can black smoulder? But that's what his eyes do.

Then he side-steps so that he's behind a cracked pane. It's as if I see him through a kaleidoscope. His face is split and shattered and pulled every which way.

He vanishes, but my heart goes on fluttering.

He's not with today's Hysterical Holidaymakers, so who is he?

He's different. He's like a ghost drifting round the edges of our world, but his eyes reach mine and I cannot look away.

6
The weird couple

Dear Brother

'Orrible onion soup. And then grey lumpy stew. I'm getting so slim, slim enough to fade away! So why doesn't it work on Mrs Silk? She must pig out in secret. I tell you, Mrs Silk could double as a Bouncy Castle. Work hard, Student Sam.

Rachel

I suppose you'd call Mr and Mrs Silk a couple. Why?

Because they are called Mr and Mrs Silk.

What is a couple anyway? I know *our* parents were a couple, Sam, I've seen photos of them with long hair, no bald bits or wrinkles. I remember them holding hands when they watched sad telly; *University Challenge*, Monty Python, *E.R.* Programmes we don't bother with, Sam. (I talk away to you in my head sometimes. It helps.)

I can't really talk to anyone here.

I talk to Beth a bit sometimes, really to find out if I'm going mad or not.

'Do you think there's anyone else living here?' I ask her, now that I've seen a ghost. Twice.

She frowns. 'There's just the Silks and Robbie,' she says.

Robbie? Robbie has a job here working the machinery for the visitors to watch. He is called the Overseer. Only adults should work the machines, says Mr Silk, not us.

Beth flirts with Robbie all the time. It's obvious she wants to be an item with Robbie the Overseer.

'I suppose there isn't another Overseer?' I try. 'I mean, you haven't seen anyone else?'

'No I *haven't*,' she frowns.

So, back to the Silks, and the question: What is a couple?

Mr and Mrs Silk are a real mismatch. Mr Silk is tall and hawk-like. I can't see him easily in my mind, but I know he's always smiling. The smile flits around his lips. He's pale. So maybe he's more a vulture than a hawk? Maybe that's nasty, Rachel, I hear you say . . .

Mrs Silk is small and round. She is what Auntie Flo would call '*a homely little body*'. She has little lips in a round face and brown hair pulled back into a bun. She dresses up in long skirts of black and whirs along as if she is on casters. (I know! She's a Dalek!)

In the mornings Mrs Silk teaches us for an hour in the

schoolroom. It's all a performance for the parties of visitors and is supposed to make us role-play cotton apprentices. We have chalk and slates. I ask you!

'We're not quite historically accurate,' says Mrs Silk. 'Maths and writing were taught on Sundays, when the apprentices were not at work. And then only boys were taught.' This produced a mock moan of, '*Shame!*' from the girls.

Mrs Silk looks disapproving. I think she wishes it was still like that, with girls barred from the schoolroom. So do I.

At least I'm not wearing that cotton bonnet today. I lost it, oh dear me! Mrs Silk notices that my hair is held up with combs. They're my favourite hair furniture; they're purple, dusted with silver.

'My bonnet fell off when I was leaning over the wheel pit,' I tell her. 'It will have been all churned up by now.'

She purses her lips and says, 'I'll bring you another from the laundry later on. The Master did want you all to look perfect! He wants the mill to be as authentic as it can. He is such a perfectionist!'

Her eyes gleam at the thought of her husband. She's potty about him.

It takes all sorts.

In Mrs Silk's lessons we pretend we are learning by rote. We chant tables and the alphabet. The visitors stand and stare. I feel so stupid, a parrot in a long skirt, but at least I'm bonnet-less.

We're going to do needlework. If there's one thing I hate, it's sewing. We're going to make a sampler for the wall. 'Home Sweet Home', perhaps, 'Spooks Rule OK' . . .

The visitors love all these little touches. They love the spidery writing in the 'sick book' with the old-fashioned ailments. They love the list of *sins* on the wall:

> *Sticking out tongues at the Overseer*
> *Throwing bobbins*
> *Falling asleep at work*
> *Running away*

That last one sounds good: *running away, running as fast as your feet can carry you, over the hills and far away from Phoney Phantom Folly!*

How were the real 'prentices punished? They lost their bread and dripping. That would be fine by me, but if that's all you got to eat, it would be real retribution.

'Didn't they get beaten, Mrs Silk?' asks a boy eagerly, hoping for horror stories.

'I think they did sometimes, I'm afraid,' she says. 'But don't worry. We won't beat you!'

After the schoolroom session the others charge across the courtyard to the day-room and the drinks machine.

I wander off the other way. I just want to get away from them all. With a quick glance over my shoulder, I scramble up a stone wall and pull myself over.

In my head I hear Miss Benson's voice. If a group of us is mucking around, she only sees *me*. She snaps, 'Rachel! Don't be silly, Rachel. You never think first, do you?'

I drop down. It's further this side and it's a shock because I land in something cold and wet. Eugh! I'm in mud, I'm almost in the pond. It wasn't a lake of black glass we saw that first day. It was the millpond.

There's long wet grass which soaks my legs and the bottom of my stupid skirt. I come to a pile of stones and rubble, bits of rusting metal and broken glass. I climb carefully over it. Here's another stone building. I clump along by the wall, squelching with each step, round the corner and see a door standing open.

7

This one's no princess

It's gloomy inside as if it's full of fog, but I can hear things. There's a low humming sound, a rattling like little hailstones, and singing.

It's a pretty tune, and I'm sure I recognise it. Of course! We sang it at junior school.

> *Row, row, row your boat*
> *Gently down the stream*
> *Merrily, merrily, merrily now*
> *Life is but a dream.*

A sweet, busy singing above the humming of the machine.

I'm almost upon her before I see her. A shaft of sunlight glances down from the tall windows and puts a halo round her head.

She's standing there, a little figure with a head of gold.

Through my memory dance ghosts, fairies and the princess trying to spin gold from straw in *Rumpelstiltskin*.

But this one's no princess. She's filthy-dirty. Her arms and legs are bird-bone thin. But that hair! It's beautiful. It's a sunburst.

She sings merrily and I see her hands are full of thread. I clear my throat. No response, so I cough dramatically and she turns her head to look at me. Her face is heart-shaped and her skin creamy-white as the climbing rose Mum planted by the garage, but her mouth droops a little at one side and her right eye is odd, a bit bulgy. She stares at me for a moment and then covers the eye with her hand.

I have a memory of something similar, hiding away. It won't come out. I don't want it to, I don't want it spiralling up to the surface.

'Hello,' she says.

'Hello,' I say. 'I'm Rachel.'

She nods and smiles and waits, hand still over her eye like a white patch. Her other eye is blue as a cornflower.

Her clothes are worn thin and shiny. Threads hang from her shawl. This is how the mill children must have looked a couple of hundred years ago, and I wonder if I'm in some kind of time slip.

Try again. I say, 'I'm Rachel Williamson. I'm here for a holiday.'

'My goodness gracious.' Her voice is halting, almost as if

it's computer generated. 'A hol-i-day. A holiday today?'

A holiday that seems like for ever. 'It's just a few days. What's your name?' I ask.

'Sally.'

I wait. She's not going to offer any surname.

'I'm from Nottingham,' I say. 'Where are you from, Sally?'

'I am from here!' she says, as if it's obvious.

'Where's here?'

'The mill, of course. I'm here all the time.'

She speaks as if that's something to be proud of, her head tilted.

She takes her hand away from the bulgy eye, picks up hanks of cotton and shows them to me. There are pails of liquid on the stone floor.

'They're from onion skins,' she says, 'and, look! That one has woad. It makes colours like the sky . . .' She feeds the hanks of cotton into the buckets, leaving the end draped over the rim. She asks, 'Are you from a mill in Nott-Notty–'

'Nottingham. No. I'm not from a mill. I don't think there are many cotton-mills there, but they make lace. And there's a castle, a big castle on a hill with cannons.'

'I like castles!' she cries. 'You can get princesses there. Up towers. Like Rapunzel.'

'Yes, you'd like Nottingham Castle. I live in a house. You should come and see me, Sally. It's number 123 . . .'

'I can do the numbers,' she cries. 'And I can write my name. Daniel taught me.'

'Who's Daniel? Is he your brother?' I ask.

She shrugs.

Her hair dazzles! Sometimes you see photographs of forests with a sun splintered in the treetops, and her hair looks like that.

'Where are your parents, Sally?'

'Dunno.'

I can't leave it alone. 'Is Mr Silk your father, Sally?'

She glances at me, her eyes so wide that I know it's fear. I feel bad, as if I've touched something painful. I want to cover it up again and so I say, trying to sound bright and breezy, 'I've got a father called Mike. And a big brother called Sam. He's at college all day.'

She says, 'I like those things in your hair.'

'Have one,' I say, reaching up for a comb but –

'No!' growls a voice that makes me start.

It's *him*.

He's standing in the shadows at the foot of a staircase, an iron spiral that disappears into the darkness.

Sally's face lights up in a smile and she scurries across to him. She turns to look at me. I think it's pride on her face. Sort of, *look, he's with me, he's mine!*

'What are you doing here, Daniel?' she asks.

He looks down at her fondly.

'I've been watching the ginger tom play with a mouse. He caught it and juggled with it. Then he looked away and washed his paws. The mouse thought it had got its freedom. It had almost escaped when *wham* the cat pounced again. And again . . .'

'What happened to the little mouse, Daniel?' she whispers.

'I snatched it from the cat. I twirled it by its little tail and threw it in the millpond. Wheee! It's a much quicker end that way.'

He looks at me as if to say, want to make something of it?

I feel a bit sick at the thought of the mouse spinning in the air. I know that's what he wants.

He's much taller than Sally. I can't tell how old she is, maybe not much younger than I am, but he is more. He's older than I am and his skin is milky brown, the colour my dad likes his tea. He could do with a shave. He is swarthy. (I don't remember using that word before.) Wild gypsy hair, dark brows. So fit. So handsome. So hostile.

He's in his own world. He's separate, with his own atmosphere, dark and storm-racked. He says to me, 'You shouldn't be here. You shouldn't be talking to her,' and I wonder if they're ghosts. Whether they are real or not. Either way, there are so many questions I'm not sure I want to ask . . .

And his voice is low and full. There is so much of it, as if it comes from a cavern deep inside him.

He says, 'Come, Sally.'

He takes Sally's hand and leads her up the iron staircase.

After a little while I hear a door boom shut.

8

Someone else is watching

Dear Sam
I don't like it here. It's unreal. I think there are two
ghosts. All right, Sam. I've told you about the ghosts
after all.

Rachel

I've still got the postcards I've written for you, Sam. There isn't anywhere to buy stamps, and there isn't a postbox, which is a bit silly for a holiday centre.

I haven't slept very well. The box bed in the dormitory is comfortable. It's not eighteenth-century straw jumping with fleas. The bed has a duvet with a floral cover, two pillows and a soft mattress, and I'm warm enough. But I'm a city girl. It's so silent here at night. I picture the world outside, a vast black void. A fierce river. Great bony trees, like those candlesticks they use at Jewish Sabbath. We saw some in R.S. years back.

I don't think I like the countryside. I feel as if I don't know it. Yesterday in the yard something with a silver lurex sausage for a tail darted past my feet. A real country squirrel! There must be rats. Lots of rats with horrible tails, despite the ginger tom. I've seen him prowl through the yard. He's big, more like a lynx than a house cat.

There are bats. There's an owl. I don't like to hear it.

I wish Wally was with me. I want to bury my face in his hearth-rug back.

In the darkness I can picture the buildings. I know buildings, they have a familiar shape. But I can't imagine the hills and dales. They're all earth and stone and darkness! No bricks, or beams. There's too much of them. They terrify me.

All night, it seems, I listen to the river racing, and another sound. It takes a while for me to work out that it is rain, heavy rain, a downpour.

The river will rise. We will all be flooded. I want to go home. *Now*.

I fall into heavy black sleep.

Mr Silk welcomes us in this morning. He's so charming and courteous. The benefactor, the entrepreneur, with a little trace of Basil Fawlty, I think.

He's such a show-off. When we went swimming yesterday evening he said he wouldn't be coming. 'Water is not my element,' he smirked and pretended to flounder around and drown, so that everyone screeched with laughter, except

44

me. Why can't he just say he can't swim? Why is he so pompous?

Mrs Silk's face fell when he said he wasn't coming. She looked let down.

I find Mr Silk creepy. I don't know why.

He stands with his hands behind his back so that his big shoulders are like folded wings. I see his wide mouth with a gleam of teeth and think of the sluicegate.

'Good morning, Narrow Dale Mill!' he cries. 'Now then . . . I have a surprise for all you 'prentices. Look!'

And from behind his back he whips out a stick. He plucks it back and lets it go. TWANG! We all flinch in spite of ourselves.

Mr Silk throws back his head and laughs. He cries, 'See? I'm a magician. That's my wand! I cut it from the hazel bushes on the daleside.'

He leans forward, conspiratorially. 'I believe that some mill masters used their sticks on their apprentices. To punish them.' He runs his fingers slowly down the stick again. TWANG! It slices the air.

'I bet it hurt, don't you?' he says.

Next to me Beth is laughing like a drain. I steal a look at everyone else. They think he's a stand-up comedian. He bows and smiles, and goes.

'You're so twitchy, Rachel,' says Beth when I tell her that Silk gives me the creeps. 'Lighten up, won't you, girl?'

We're doing block printing. Is this infant school, or what?

Now, I've done silkscreen printing in art. I loved it. I loved stretching the silk across the wooden frame, cutting the stencil and squeegee-ing the different inks. Each layer adds something more. Each print is a surprise. You never know what you're really getting. The image is fluid; it changes constantly from what you saw the last time. I wanted to make a cushion cover for Mum. I used colours that made me shiver: bronze and peacock-green and indigo. It was supposed to be an iris, her favourite flower. I know because when I was about ten I saved up and bought her a bunch of tall irises, deep blue and purple crests of velvet, and she cried.

The inks spread and spread on my silk cushion cover and it didn't look quite like the proud flower I had intended. It was too thick to be lustrous; more like a blob, except where the colours thinned and diffused. But she said it was wonderful, unique, precious (she went on and on, almost too much) and that the cushion was for the back of the sofa because it was far too nice to sit on.

In Mrs Silk's schoolroom I'm supposed to sit with a couple of younger children and help them. If there's one thing this holiday experience has taught me, it's that I don't want to work with children. Ever. They're eleven and twelve but they ask for things all the time and squabble and tell tales on each other and moan.

Actually, I'm enjoying my printing. We cut a pattern into a soft wood block. The younger ones glue on some string to make a relief pattern, because that's supposed to be easier. (Not for the pains on my table. I have to help them and get all glued up.)

I'm cutting a floral design: Lilies of the valley and those little red bleeding heart flowers that tremble on thin stems.

I'm happy while I'm doing this. I don't think about anything else. I wonder if the apprentices ever lost themselves and their worries in work? I wonder whether a robin might be nice, a long-legged body among the flowers. The colouring could be tricky.

I'm musing on this when I see her.

It could never be anyone else with that hair. She must have crept in without being seen and she's hovering at the back. I'm just about to shout, 'Sally!' when it occurs to me I shouldn't. I hear swishing. I think Mrs Silk is standing up (it's hard to tell). I *did* see Sally, didn't I? Sally vanishes.

Mrs Silk swishes over the floor, her black skirts spreading like hot tar across a road. She stares at the space where Sally has been. She's just not sure . . .

Head down quick; mustn't let her know I've seen Sally. Maybe Sally was looking for me? I leave it as long as I can bear to, and then get up and walk quietly to the door.

Mrs Silk is next to me at once, no footsteps to be heard.

'Where are you going, Rachel?' she simpers.

47

'Toilet,' I whisper. 'It's *that* time, Mrs Silk . . . you know . . .'

I'm a liar, but a good one! What can she say? She pats my shoulder, woman to woman, and says, 'Be quick, then. We'd like to get the blocks finished this morning.'

I don't head straight for the loo. Sally won't have gone that way, I'm sure. I hesitate and then hurry through the mill, in and out of the silent machines.

And there she is. Standing quite still, humming to herself. There's a lamp on the wall behind and it edges her in gold.

I'm just about to call out to her when I realise someone else is watching.

He creeps up behind her. He doesn't wear clogs. He wears high boots of soft leather. He whistles softly. Sally stops and so does he, stroking his hazel wand across his palm.

He has a fire outline round his head from the lamp on the wall.

'Sally!' he whispers. 'Sall-eee! Shall we play chase, my dear?'

And she was off, dancing away from him. She dodges the machines, flitting in and out like a trapped butterfly. She must have played this game before.

Mr Silk isn't playing properly. He is humouring her.

She has no chance. She twists and turns and dodges. Silk waits. He's a cobra.

Suddenly he strikes. He catches her wrist.

He lifts up his switch, pauses to savour the second of anticipation, then brings it down SMACK! on the wall. I see Sally's slight body flinch. He brings it down again SMACK! SMACK! against the stone.

I flinch, and gasp. I feel as if I'm Sally and the switch is beating me, and then in slow-motion I see another Silk hitting her white neck and shoulders.

Did I cry out?

For a split second his head twitches in my direction. He's half smiling and now I see his eyes. They are so pale. Pale grey as pebbles flecked with white. They are dead. I don't think they see me.

I feel as if he's dragging out my insides.

He pulls Sally outside and away from me.

I only hear her feet sliding on the stone.

9

Not my kind of paradise

Perhaps I'm making it all up? Having hallucinations? Perhaps this isn't happening at all? Or I just see things differently from everybody else. I haven't seen Sally today at all. Or Daniel.

Robbie the Overseer also drives a minibus. (Perhaps it should be called a millibus?) He drives us all for a day out at Paradise Park, with Beth gazing at him misty-eyed from the front seat. It's noisy after Narrow Dale, screams and engines and pop music. Everywhere is thick with the smell of fast food, caramelised onions, burgers dripping with ketchup, bendy pizzas and baked potatoes that taste grey.

The crowds surge against us, intent on squeezing the last little drop of a good time from their day out. And there's temper, my goodness there's bad temper! There's smacking and snapping and infants bawling and parents shouting, *'Wait till I get you home!'*

I blame the queues. The queues for the Ghost House, Mystical Maze, the Great Wheel of Fate, the Kamikaze Kastle and the Ferry to Hades are endless.

Now, I'm a coward. I have a sit on the Giant Spider and a go on the Crocodile, but I draw a line at most rides. All right, so I'm a spoilsport, a mouldy fig. Maybe given the right company, enough sleep and food, I'd like it, and I'd have a go on almost everything. Instead I munch my candyfloss (neon pink and yellow), and try not to think of the dentist.

Paradise Park. It's not *my* kind of paradise.

Beth bounces up to me. 'Look at this teddy-bear Robbie won for me on the rifle range!' she shrieks.

'Nice,' I mutter. The teddy is pink with black plastic spectacles. Eugh.

'See that kiosk?' she cries. 'I'm getting my mum a present from there.'

It's the Narrow Dale Mill kiosk. You can buy tickets for a visit. There is a picture of an apprentice with a round apple face and a smear of muck on his nose. Children who want to play poor 'prentices at home can nag their sulking parents into buying them the gear: snow-white cotton smocks and bonnets, long skirts and baggy trousers. There are clogs shiny as conkers. There are slates with sticks of chalk, tins of Narrow Dale Winter Broth and Mill Master's Treacle Toffee.

Then I see the thread. There are skeins of cotton thread

for sale, '*hand-crafted at every process*.' It doesn't say hand-crafted by Sally. The colours are so pretty, so soft and unworldly, they make my mouth water. There is sunflower yellow and acorn brown, raspberry pink and forget-me-not blue.

'My mum would like those,' cries Beth. 'She does embroidery pictures. You know, it's all drawn out and you just follow the lines. She makes cushion covers. I'll buy some for her.'

The skeins of blue thread are beautiful. Speedwell blue, harebell, cornflower, delphinium, iris . . . I can't stop looking at them. I won't be buying any. Instead I buy chocolate. Lots. It's Give-yourself-bad-skin Day. I feel depressed. I want to punish myself.

Perhaps I'm making it all up, or having hallucinations. She was terrified! It was a horrible game Mr Silk played with her, if it *was* a game.

No one else seems to notice anything. Not even Mrs Silk.

Mrs Silk is in charge this afternoon, in so-called normal clothes, all drab and droopy. Mr Silk is nowhere to be seen. Why? What's he doing? Shouldn't he be with his group of visitors? (I'm a curious girl, always have been. Sam says I'm nosey.)

One good thing about Paradise Park: it has different postcards! There are cards with cuddly creatures; you know, koalas and chimps that look like they're smiling, and there are ostriches and puppies and fluffy kittens. I find the perfect card for Sam.

There's a postbox, but no stamp machine.

On the way back Mrs Silk is on edge. She squirms and clears her throat and keeps glancing at her watch. It's late when we get back.

Suddenly there's the mill, rushing up from the earth into the darkness. I think I'd secretly hoped it might vanish while we were out. It looks even worse. I wonder if the Silks have considered renting it out for a film set, you know, *Psycho 15*, *Addams Family Dynasty*, *Giant Silk Worms Take Over The World*.

I look up hoping to see *him* at a window. No such luck. The days are skimming past and I want to get to know him. I've never seen anyone quite like him before.

In the mill's face the window eyes are lit yellow. I wonder how it was in the past, in the days before electricity.

I don't need to wonder. I can see how it was. The far building is in total darkness, except for a small window, right at the top, where a little light flickers.

10
Daniel

Here are their headlights. They are back.

They are to stay here again tonight, then. And the girl? The girl who talks to Sally?

She must be with them.

She is looking for trouble!

Sally is taken with her and talks of her all the time. It's no wonder. She has known no other girls.

She has only been with *me*. Mr and Mrs Silk, and me. I made her.

The candles cast yellow globes against the walls. When we were younger I would hold a candle under my face and be a demon! How Sally screamed . . .

I have always been here, in this place of stone. How many months of my life have I spent in this window, thinking this is all the world there is? Now it seems to me that there may be another world, the world the visitors come from.

They are not adults, like Mr and Mrs Silk. Some of them are younger then Sally! And yet how different from Sally they are . . . Tonight the river is full and loud, as it was that night Sally was first brought here. The Silk-wife bustled about and clucked and cooed around the girl child. Mr Silk was silent. He would not let the little girl sleep by his wife at night. She was left in that little room to cry until she had no crying left. That night, at least . . .

I was puzzled by this girl child. She did not like the loudness of the water. She clapped her hands upon her ears. She could hardly speak, then.

I taught her. I taught her 'water', 'river', 'dale', 'hungry'.

Then Mrs Silk, fussing whenever *he* would let her, gave Sally a picture book. It had a dark blue cover with gold writing on the spine – *Sunny Stories for Small Folk*.

Sally pored over that book. She loved one picture especially, a picture of Paradise in pink and white and blue. An apple-cheeked lady smiled out from the doorway of a little thatched cottage. Roses scrambled across the white-washed walls. Hollyhocks speared a blue sky behind and a stream burbled under an arched bridge. A brown cow gazed thoughtfully out at the reader, a buttercup sticking out of its mouth.

'That's the country, Sally,' I told her. She frowned and ran to the window. She pointed out at the closed dale and the sliver of grey sky.

'No country,' she said.

That was the first time I ever really looked out of the window. That has been the whole world for us, that view and the mill. A river has cut the dale out of rock, a dale as dim and hidden as the pucker on Sally's brow. The river is hard and angry. *Mr Silk calls the water 'soft'.* He's wrong. The river rages through the secret dale, hurling everything out of its way. When we were small Mrs Silk would take us for walks by the glimmering reeds and up the dale, and point out to us the things that grew there. As we grew older, these walks ceased.

Mr Silk is the first thing I remember, tall and dark as something stepped off a grave in a cemetery. There are shadows behind him, but I can't remember who they were.

Mrs Silk came near, caring for me as she was allowed, but *he* was Master, and was Sally's master too when she came here. He would not let his Silk-wife cuddle us in his sight.

He told me that Sally was 'the idiot child'. He said that the eighteenth-century dealers brought one idiot in every batch of twenty orphans to the mill owners. They were cheap, I suppose. They could work hard and not ask for much in return.

'Sally is not an idiot,' I said.

Then Mr Silk sneered at me. 'How would you know, Daniel? How would you know who is, and who isn't, an idiot?'

Because I know Sally. She is, simply, Sally. She gets all in a muddle. She can't always find her words. Sometimes she calls her straw mattress a 'loaf' – and says words the wrong way round, like, 'You're dandsome, Haniel!'

She has headaches, her right eye doesn't work properly, she loses things and cries.

Once I shouted, 'Why are you so stupid, Sally?'

She just smiled at me and said, 'I was hit on the head by a star, Danny. I was, I was! It wiped away my memory. Like I wipe the slate for my ABC.'

And I have taught her everything she knows. Simple Sally. She has a happiness that came from somewhere else. It is a constant light inside her. She has shone all these years for me, she is the light of my life.

I cannot help but tease her. I call her names. I call her Wall-eye, Sally Stupid, Carrot-hair, Chuckle-head. She laughs at me.

Somewhere long ago I had a book of nursery rhymes. There were pictures. One of the pictures was a sun. It had golden rays that streamed out like Sally's hair.

> *Sally go round the sun.*
> *Sally go round the moon.*
> *Sally go round the chimneypots*
> *On a Saturday afternoon.* (Or was it a *Sunday* afternoon . . . Monday morning?)

*

Tonight, Sally is gone a long time and I don't know where *he* is, and that makes it worse. Everything, our whole world, is disturbed. The Silks have other children *staying* here! They are not just visiting in the middle of the day and then disappearing in a car. We are used to keeping well away from visitors. None have stayed at night before.

He has told us to leave them well alone. He told me, 'Sally will be punished if you don't keep to yourselves.' Sally keeps wanting to see them.

I have spied on them from the walkway. They have funny clothes and strange hair and most of them are fat. There's that girl who turns her face this way in curiosity. I saw her first through the glass. Her face is shaped as pretty as a new beech leaf, with wide cheekbones and her chin tip-tilted. Her mouth is small and pink as a bud.

This girl's eyes are dark and full as pools, full of secrets. And questions, too. She knows we are here. She knows something about me. She brings trouble.

The door opens. In trails Sally, her shawl wrapped tight round her head and tied under her chin. I'll pretend nothing is wrong, although I know it is. It's like poking a stick at a kitten. I don't know why I want to goad her, when her eyes shine so with tears.

'Sit down, Sally,' I tell her, 'and take off your shawl.'

'No,' she says. There is a big lump in her cheek. Barley

sugar. Silk often feeds her sweeties after he has made her weep, and weep she surely has.

So I'll make it better, I'll make her laugh! I stalk up and down in front of her, pronouncing in a great deep voice, 'I am Mr Silk, all you common-as-muck folk! I am very important with my great big mill! I talk on and on and on, and I go to swank around and show off giving talks to worthy gentlemen while they eat their big grand dinners! Whoops!'

This is the bit she loves – I slip on a pretend banana skin and lie on the floor.

I sneak a little look at Sally. Her sobs are changing to giggles. That's what I want.

'Help! Mr La-Di-Da Bigbum Silk here, I'm in the river, help! I'm carried away down the dale on to the rocks and far away!' I bellow.

Sally splutters, 'Stop it, Danny, stop it! I'll wet meself!'

I'm up and quick as a flash undo the knot of shawl at her throat. I hold it at arm's length in front of her and let it drop in a swirl on the floor. Sally tries to sink her head down into her body like a tortoise hiding in its shell. Too late. Now I see.

Rage rushes up through my chest and head.

He's cut off her hair. A great thick golden ray of hair. So that she seems to have hair on only one side of her head. Without the golden halo shining all round it, Sally's face looks more like a moon than the sun. Sally's hair inflames him. It turns him mad.

She whimpers, 'Look at my arms, Daniel. Look at the red marks. Why does Mr Silk do these things to us, Danny? Is it what grown-ups do?'

'How should I know, Sally? I don't know *why*.'

I read in a book once that people are cruel if they've had unhappy lives.

I don't know anything about Mr Silk's life. I don't think he was a child. I only know the man. I don't know why he does these things.

Who cares about the reason? Even if there is one. Who cares why?

The oil-lamp casts a pool of light as yellow as butter. It falls on Sally's doll. Baldy Stump Betty. Betty is her favourite doll, made from a wooden spoon. She has orange wool for hair and no arms or legs. Sally loves her dearly, so I pick her up and tuck her in the crook of Sally's arm.

'Go to your room now and sleep, Sally. Betty will look after you.'

'Daniel, perhaps I'll have that mother dream,' she whispers. 'You know. When my mother sits by the fire and sings to me. She wears clothes like Mrs Tiggywinkle in that book. But she hasn't got hedgehog prickles, Danny.'

She smiles suddenly, radiantly and I have a shudder of hatred through me as Silk's smug face rears up in front of my eyes. He's always there. He has more lives than one, I believe. I want to put my hands tight round his throat and shut my own eyes, and squeeze . . .

Mrs Silk isn't our mother. She would wish to be, but she isn't. Sally and I tell each other tales of our mothers. I say that mine had a skin like a peach and ate strawberries all day long. I had a father who showed me how to carve wood. Sally's mother made blackberry jam. Both of us know we are telling tales.

It has always been the same, and all the years stretch before us like endless steps of stone.

11
'I want to come home now'

Dear Sam

Hope you like the axolotls on this card. They make me want to throw up. I got this card at Paradise Park. Makes a change from photos of the mill. I saw a beating here. The mill man hurting a girl. I've had enough here. I want to come home now, Sam. Today I'm going to find out the truth.

Love

Rachel

I spend a little time on my looks. I'll wear my red top and black skirt. My skirt is my shortest but it's been a good summer and my legs are quite tanned. My skin is like the Himalayas today, rippling mountain ranges of spots, and so I put on make-up, plenty of it. Hope it looks like not much at all. So-oh subtle. Hair washed and worn loose. Passion flower body spray. I look again. Eugh! Try to cover up the spots with an animal-friendly conceal stick. Soft rose lipstick; nothing too garish.

As I cross the courtyard I am aware of him in the shadows.

He is always taller than I think. He's quite still. He looks at me. His expression does not change. He always has that half-smile on his face. He makes me feel awkward. He's in a suit, not his frock coat. Anyway, that frock coat is man-made stuff, I think nastily; rayon, cheap tat stuff, not real silk.

A really odd thing happens, a trick of the light perhaps. It's as if another Mr Silk, and another, then three or four more, begin to step out from behind him. They are cut-outs, as if he's being animated for some film.

I give my head a little shake and look again. Of course there is only one man there, thank goodness. I almost trip up on a cobblestone and laugh foolishly, because he is watching.

Later that day, Mrs Silk is in a jolly mood.

'The Master is away to Buxton this evening,' she tells us, her little eyes dancing. 'He is addressing members of the local history society. The Mayor and the press will be there! It's an after-dinner speech, children. Just look at the menu.'

She waves a white and gold card with copperplate writing.

> *Grilled Camembert with green salad*
> *Summer tomato soup*

Quail with new potatoes and fresh vegetables
Truite aux amandes with sauté potatoes and petit pois
Chocolate profiteroles and fresh cream
Gingered fruit salad with lemon sorbet
Coffee. Dark chocolate mints.

Blimey! Double chocolate profiteroles for me, please.

There *can't* be anything wrong with Mr Silk, or someone would know, wouldn't they? The Mayor or someone. Giving after-dinner speeches? He's so respected.

'Didn't you want to go, Mrs Silk?' asks Beth, tactful as ever.

Mrs Silk's cheek pouches pinken. 'Oh no, dear. He is a man of such standing.'

I feel sorry for her. 'Has Mr Silk always been so – so –' I stop myself saying *obsessed* '– so fascinated by mills?'

'Oh yes, Rachel. He should be living two hundred years ago!'

I think he is.

She says, 'We will cook a fine meal for ourselves, such as the wealthy mill owners might have eaten long ago. Not the potato broth and oat porridge eaten by the poor 'prentices, oh no! Only the best! Rachel? Aren't you cold in that little skirt, Rachel?'

'No,' I lie.

So we set to and prepare our fine meal. I haven't done

real cooking for months now, haven't wanted to. We beat batter for Yorkshire pudding. We prepare onion gravy with a dash of Worcester sauce in it. We wash potatoes to roast in the range and slice crisp cabbage, crinkly as tight contours on a map. It's pretty but I bet it's left over afterwards.

We core big apples and fill the bore holes with raisins, brown sugar and cinnamon. We stick them round with cloves so that they turn into green pomanders. There are big bowls of yellow cream to beat until just more than floppy.

Mrs Silk is smiling. She's relaxed tonight. Her little face is rosy from the range and I wonder if I'm mistaken about her, about everything. Perhaps I'm imagining things? Shall I ask her about Sally and Daniel, does she know about them? She *must* do. Surely.

But I have to find out for myself.

'Would you like to help with the beef, Rachel?' asks Mrs Silk.

'No thank you,' I whisper. 'Normally I would love to cook beef,' (big lie) 'but I'm still feeling unwell. I think I'll lie down until supper, if that's all right.'

'Of course, my dear,' she says, concern in her voice. I feel her eyes follow me to the door. (I feel as if Miss Benson is watching me too, sneers all over her face. Guilt, guilt.)

I make a big show of stumbling up our stairs, just in case Mrs Silk is watching me. At the top I wait a moment then dart back and go outside.

I slip away to that wall and scramble up to the top. This time I *look* before I drop the other side. Just as well. There's no way I can get to Sally's staircase that way. The night rain has made the millpond even deeper and it's flooded right over the bank. It was difficult the last time I went this way. I had to clean my stupid clogs and dry my mill-girl's skirt. I think I'd have to swim today. I could nip round the end of the building, I think, but that's right next to the pond and I might be seen. So I'll try to reach them a different way. I go outside the mill, through those big iron gates and along the road that leads back to the real world. I hope no one thinks I'm doing a runner.

On one side of the road there's a steep wood with those Sabbath candlestick trees. On the other side is a stone wall, the wall round the mill. I edge over it and tramp across wasteland, cursing the wet grass and stinging my legs on nettles.

I'm just going down a slope when I hear a terrible noise, a sort of angry grunting squealing noise! *What is it?*

An enormous white beast with no eyes and no fur is thundering after me, pulling lots of little beasts behind it as if they're on strings!

Help! I flounder through the grass, hurl myself at another wall and fall down the other side. The beast skids and stops short.

It's a pig. I didn't know pigs could be so big, or so fast. Its piglets seize the chance to re-clamp on to its teats. Mum and I saw some pigs in Suffolk once, *nice* pigs. They had a pig city with rows of round-roofed houses, like Nissen huts.

I'm soaked. I've landed in a little garden. I can smell damp, dug earth, and green stuff rotting. There's cabbage, I know that one, and there are other leafy things in rows. Onions push pale golden globes above the dark earth. Old-fashioned marigolds glow amongst the vegetables and I can smell mint, fresh on the air.

But there's a horror scarecrow! It's leaning over to one side. I'm not sure I've ever seen a real scarecrow before. This one is all dressed up with one of Mr Silk's flamboyant C&A frock coats. It has bleached hanks of cotton for hair and no eyes.

A little robin is pecking at the soil.

There's a gate. I let myself through and I'm on cobble-stones. Instinct tells me that if I go to the left and round the building I'll come to that door again. It's difficult, because the millpond is almost level with my feet and there's hardly any bank to walk on.

Just when I get really scared I come to the door. It's closed. Well, I've got this far so I might just as well turn the handle. It's locked.

No it's not. It's just stiff. It opens.

I put my hand inside and feel the wall but there's no light switch. My heart is thudding fast but I *know* those crouching shapes are looms. They can't hurt me. On the windowsill near the door is a candle stub in a holder and a bundle of matches. My hands shake but I light it at last. Wee Willie Winkie never had this trouble! I clank up the iron steps as if I'm a ghost dragging my chains. To keep myself going I chant the rhyme.

> Wee Willie Winkie
> Runs through the town
> Upstairs and downstairs
> In his night-gown.
> Hammer on the front door
> Holler through the lock
> 'Is everybody safely home?
> It's past eight o'clock.'

Or something like that. It's a long time since I heard it.

Here's the top.

I'm in one of those films on telly late at night, the films your parents don't want you to watch. Silly people, usually blonde and female, go creeping around old houses, fingertip touching creaky doors. Why do they do it?

Because you want them to.

And the door is open.

12

'Is Sally all right?'

They're both here, up in this attic.

It's full of candles, like a side-chapel in a cathedral.

Daniel stands scowling by the window. Sally moves nearer
to him, pulling her shawl over her head, but not before I've
seen what's happened.

Someone has hacked her hair off above her ear. Only
on one side. The other side still tumbles down as bright
as gold.

She looks odder than ever now it is cut so unevenly. She
looks unbalanced.

Daniel glares at me.

'You're in the wrong part of the mill,' he says. His voice is
like someone stirring gravel with their toe. It sends shivers
down my spine. 'You shouldn't be here at all.'

'A pig chased me.'

'I like the pigs,' cries Sally. 'We have to clean them out.

And then in the winter, we hear – we hear –' she screws up her face.

'We hear them screaming when he sticks them,' says Daniel, watching me for a reaction. He's not going to get one. 'I'll do the slaughtering one day soon.'

He looks down at Sally and says, 'Did you come here to-die? No, I came here yester-die.'

She giggles and says, 'Same old corny jokes, Danny.'

I say, 'I just came to see if Sally was all right.'

'So you know her name?'

'It's not Rumpelstiltskin, is it? Where I have to guess a name. It's not a fairytale, is it?'

He says, 'Fairytales show things as they really are. Why shouldn't Sally be all right?'

Awkward silence. I stare at his black boots. They'd be nice if they were clean.

I look up but he's scowling at my legs. I wish I wasn't wearing such a silly short skirt. Oh no! My legs are all red and white nettle bumps.

I sort of wish he'd stop staring at me. I've never felt like this before, as if he can see right into me and all about me. I feel awkward and foolish. He *can't* be their son. I don't see how Mr and Mrs Silk, the Vulture and the Dalek, could make anything so tall, dark and gorgeous. So who is he?

I mumble, 'I came to see – I mean. Is Sally all right? I saw Sally the other day. At the back of the schoolroom. She – er

– I thought you might both come on the outing to Paradise Park, but I didn't see you there.'

Sally glances up into his face, puzzled.

'Paradise, Danny?' she whispers. 'Eve with the apples and the snake?'

Daniel's voice is as rough as scree. 'No, Sally, it's just a fair. We don't go on outings. We live here. We work here. Are you going soon?'

Thank you, Prince Charming! Stung, I say, 'Yes. I'm going for my supper soon. And I'm going home in a couple of days' time.'

'Home?' says Sally, but he puts his finger to his lips. He must shave, I think wildly, he has a cut on his chin, like a red crescent moon. I bet Silk makes him use one of those old razors with a strop thing to sharpen it. But how could he shave?

'There's no electricity in this building, is there?' I ask.

'No,' he says. 'It's been disconnected. Like you, eh, Sally? Disconnected.'

She sticks her tongue out at him and he grins, a wide, gorgeous grin so that his eyes are full of light and warmth, not that angry darkness.

'Yes, I'm going home soon.' I'm gabbling. 'You could come and see me.'

'We don't want to come and see you,' he says. 'Do we, Sally?'

She frowns up at him. 'Why not?'

'Because this is where we are. This is our world.'

On the table is a little jar full of marigolds and mint; a homely touch in this dark, cold attic.

'So have you always lived here? At the mill?'

'I told you, Rachel, we are mill children!' says Sally.

'Are you adopted or fostered or something?' I ask.

She cries, 'Yes!'

Daniel glowers and says nothing.

Sally looks sideways at me for a while and says, 'I like your shoes, Rachel. I like the big heels. And your – your – is it a skirt?'

'Yes,' I answer, feeling my face burn.

'My skirt is very rough,' she says. 'It scratches my legs.'

'Sally? Here,' I say, and from my pocket take some of the chocolate I bought at Paradise Park. (I never ate it all. A spot like Vesuvius is threatening my chin.)

Sally sniffs it, licks her lips and cries, 'Thank you!' then trots through a little doorway, beckoning me after her. I follow her into a tiny bedroom. A dark cupboard just for Sally. On the bed are funny dolls. She picks one up and gives it to me, proudly. A doll made from a wooden spoon. It is dressed in drab stuff with orange wool hair and a blue shawl over its head. Something about it reminds me of the Nativity plays we did when we were infants. Mum had to make me an angel cozzie with white silky stuff and tinsel. I wanted a wand but she said no . . .

The spoon-doll's face is marked with ink-blue eyes and a big hallowe'en pumpkin smile.

'I make my own dolls,' says Sally proudly. 'Mrs Silk gives me the things to do it. Real dolls cost too much. I've got one made from a scrubbing brush and some little babies made from pegs. And this one is for you, Rachel. But don't cut her hair.'

'Thank you. I'll call her Sally.'

Sally frowns and says, 'She's called Baldy Stump Betty.'

I glance behind me. Daniel has turned his back on us and is by the window. I whisper, 'I'll give you my telephone number, Sally, and you can –'

'Your what?' she cries.

'Shhh! My telephone number. Look.' I reach into my pocket for my little gold pen. What can I write on? You've got it! In my pocket is one of those wretched cards of Phantom Folly. I write my name, address and telephone number and hold it out. She takes it hesitantly, turns the card round and round, frowning, then puts it right up next to her good eye.

I suddenly know she can't read. I say, 'Rachel Williamson, 123 Cedar Road –'

'Nottyham!' she shouts and laughs, then turns to me with a wide smile that amazes me with its joyfulness. She slips the card inside her dress, puts her finger to her lips and giggles.

Back we go. I hold out my hand to Daniel and say, 'I'm Rachel Williamson.'

His face flushes dark red. He doesn't take my hand. Neither does he take the chocolate Sally breaks off for him.

He says, 'Leave us alone.'

I don't understand him. Why? And it's so cold up here.

'I had better go,' I say. 'We're cooking. Roast beef and Yorkshire pudding. And baked apples, filled with sugar and butter in the middle. You'll smell them soon, I bet.'

Too late I see the hunger on their faces and say, 'I could bring some up here for you.'

'No. Please go,' he says.

So I do.

13
Daniel's story

That girl . . . Rachel.

Why did she come here? With her chocolate and her lipstick and her talk of sugared apples? We can smell them cooking, with their syrupy middles, of course we can. The sweetness drifts up to our window. I drag Sally back from the door and will not let her run after it. She snivels for a while. I make her eat that chocolate. All of it.

She cries, 'You'll make me sick, Danny!'

Good. That will teach her. She must not desire those things, they are not for us.

She chatters on and on about Rachel, long after the key is turned in the lock that night. Her blue eyes shine as she talks of Rachel's shoes and skirt and her brother Sam.

'Rachel isn't the only one in the world,' I tell her.

That night I dream of islands. In my dream they are called the Windward Islands. They are islands bleached white as bone, floating in a turquoise sea. Green palm trees bow their heads as the islands drift away and out of sight over the blue horizon.

In their place come puddings. Meringues, pale and fluffy. Crumbles, dumplings moist with custard, hot fruit compote with vanilla and brown sugar, bread and butter pudding, golden roly-poly with red jam. Banana boats sail on a dark sea of rum, sweetness to taste long after. A meringue turns into a white shore, then a baked apple big as a moon rolls in on a wave and rests before me.

I wake up starving. It's too early for them to unlock the outside door and leave breakfast at the top of the stairs. Never meringues or roly-poly puds. Only oatcakes, thin and warped as old cork. That is what apprentices eat, with thin porridge to swell the stomach. Sometimes there is no breakfast left on the tray because the rats get there first and leave only crumbs, like Hansel and Gretel's trail through the forest.

I cross the room and stand before the window. I spend most of my life here.

The moon still hangs in the sky, a scar on its face as if someone has hurt it.

Sally's door opens. Here she comes, stumbling towards me, wrapped in her blanket against the morning chill. Together we look down at the millpond. We can just see the small paddle-steamer shape of the bird as he swims his circles and leaves his wake in the black water. He is always alone. He hoots as if his beak is a horn.

'I love that little bird,' says Sally. 'I envy him. He does not know we are unhappy, Danny, even though he is so near us.'

'It's all right, Sally, we'll be all right,' I say to soothe her.

That Rachel girl! She has made it worse. She has made Sally think we could have some other life after all. And now I wonder too. Could we?

'Do you want me to tell you a story, Sally?' I ask. I hope she'll say yes. I love to tell stories! You see I've always loved to read. I'm greedy for books and Silk leaves books for me. Even when I was little he left me books. He says he is a philanthropist and a missionary of the mind and he will not leave us in stark ignorance. As for Sally, he smiles and says there is little point. Her sight is poor. What good would it do her?

So sometimes I read aloud. We have Defoe and Dickens, Swift and Shakespeare, Perrault and the ghostly Grimm Brothers, *Wuthering Heights, Jane Eyre, The Water Babies*, with the story of the poor little climbing boy. *Sunbeam Stories. Samuel Smiles*. The Bible, even some old cookery books, with pictures to make our mouths water.

I read to Sally and tell her folktales and fairytales and tales of Mr Silk. While we eat our porridge I tell her *Goldilocks and the Three Bears*. Then she gives me her bowlful to finish.

Today she says, 'Tell me our very own story, Danny. We

are adopted, aren't we? Mr and Mrs Silk chose us, didn't they? They chose you first. Then me.'

Here I go again. I take a deep breath and begin.

'Mr and Mrs Silk went to a special parade, clutching their gold. There were lots of little girls whose mothers and fathers got lost. *Hundreds* of little girls. Princesses too. All the little girls were pretty and clever, and they could dance and sing. There was *just one* changeling child, called Sally. Mr and Mrs Silk turned their heads from side to side and could not make up their minds. But in the end they chose –'

'Sally!' she shouts and claps her hands.

'Yes, they chose Sally. Sally was the best.'

She doesn't really understand. She isn't adopted or fostered, as that Rachel suggested, damn her. She was bought. I suppose I was bought too, but I was too little to remember.

The man who sold Sally to Mr Silk called himself the Dealer. I remember his thick gold rings and his glossy black hair. He smelled of sweet oil, sickly as the smell of yellow gorse in the sun. He had gold buckles on his shoes. He grinned at me and ruffled my hair so that it hurt. He said, 'How you getting on, Danny boy? It must be years since I brought you here. And now you're getting a little sister. I'm Derek the Dealer and I bring only the very best! Like her, Danny?'

Sally ran to hide in the corner of the room. She sucked

her thumb and looked round at me. Her eye was strange.

I remember money. Piles of it. Paper money. Mr Silk rustling and counting. I remember the Dealer's eyes, so sly and slippy, never meeting mine, always sliding away like thin black slugs. He laid the money carefully in a shiny wallet and gave us sweets before he went.

And later in came Mrs Silk, and she held out her arms to Sally, crying, 'A little girl! At last!' Her face was pink with joy.

Mr Silk was staring at Sally and I saw a strange light come into his eye, even then. When he sees Sally there is a presence – or is it an emptiness? – in his look I have never seen anywhere else. A distance, a thoughtfulness. Something apart and cold. I don't know.

'Now we have two adopted children, Mistress Silk,' he said then. He didn't tell her about all the money. I remember thinking, how funny, and opening my mouth to prattle about all the counting, and then thinking better of it.

Sally's face has fallen now. She puts her hand in mine. We cannot speak, we cannot say what we think. We cannot bear it.

'One day, Sally, we will leave here. We will go to the real world. We'll escape from Narrow Dale for ever. But we must stay away from those children now or Mr Silk will – he will be so angry if we talk to them.'

'I know that, Daniel. I just wish I could see where they live. It's all right, I know there won't be a mother for me.

Will the real world have chocolate and hair slides, Danny?'

'Yes. I promise.'

My heart is beating hard. I'm lying because I don't know *what* there is in the real world. Maybe we would jump out of the frying pan and into the fire! I don't know how to be with people. Only Sally.

But now I have promised. And if you make a promise to someone else then it is twice as strong. I have offered the promise to Sally. I hold the dream out to her, as soft and light as a cloud in my hands.

And so I have to do something about it.

14

Someone is watching
me . . .

Black top, red top, strappy shoes (wore them a lot, didn't I?), nail varnish, glitter, shampoo, spot-stick . . . It's very easy packing to leave Narrow Dale Mill. I can't stuff the things in the bag fast enough! It's not as though there are any extras, only some home-made fudge from Bakewell for the folks, and a chew for Wally shaped like a chocolate eclair.

Beth is sniffing in a way that wants to be noticed.

'Never mind,' I say. 'You can come back and see Robbie again, can't you?'

'Don't know,' she blubs. 'Robbie won't say.'

'Does he work here all the time?'

'No, stupid! Only in the season. Only until the last day of October.'

'Will he work here next year as well?'

She shrugs. 'Depends what other job he gets. He says the Silks are good to work for.'

I can't believe my ears. 'But they're weird! She's – well, she's just a sad fat person. But he is a nutter. Isn't he?'

'He's a bit eccentric. That's all, Rachel.' She pulls a face at me. 'Don't be so straight and boring! He's a *character*.'

Perhaps it's me who is bonkers. Perhaps he is a character. Perhaps he is just flamboyant, and I'm used to men like my dad and sensible Sam, and not to a showman like Silk?

'Beth . . . are you sure Robbie is the only lad here at the mill?'

'*Yes*! You're the nutter, Rachel!'

'Have you seen a girl? Sort of poorly dressed? Like a mill worker from way back?'

'No I haven't! You must be seeing things.'

'And Robbie's not mentioned anything about other children here? About Mrs Silk's children.'

'Ah . . . he did say there were a couple staying here. I think they may be foster children from a home. They keep themselves to themselves and Robbie's been told not to bother them.'

She's not interested in anything other than the wretched Robbie. She says, 'Right. That's the packing finished. I'll go and find him.' She sniffs again and dabs at her eyes with a tissue. Then she picks up her rucksack and staggers off to look for her love.

I hear hooves clopping on the stones in the yard, and the snort of the great grey horse with his snow-dappled sides.

You wouldn't believe it. We are to travel back to Bakewell in the horse and cart.

Mrs Silk is there, plump face tilted in regret. It seems as if she is sad to see us go.

'Goodbye, Rachel,' she says, hands twisting the frill of her flowery apron. 'Goodbye, my dear. I hope you enjoyed yourself.'

'Yes thank you, Mrs Silk,' I say because I'm a well-brought-up girl. I must stop trying to read things hidden in her chocolate-button eyes. There's longing there. She wants to be liked.

Shrieking and whooping, the others scramble on to the cart. I wait my turn.

Someone is watching me. I know.

The skin on the back of my neck prickles as if I'm wearing a scarf of pins, points down. I know who is watching me. I don't want to turn round and see.

In the end, I cannot help myself. I turn.

Mr Silk stands by the wall. He is staring at me, I know, although his eyes are hooded. I don't want to look into his eyes.

He says, 'Rachel. Haven't you forgotten something, Rachel?'

Panic in my mind. He's smiling. He's horrible. I want to get away, fast.

He says my name again, softly. 'Rachel?'

Daniel and Sally, they must have said something to him. He makes me sick with fright. He holds out his hand.

'There. You *had* forgotten something. Something you wanted. See?'

He has my little gold pen, the one with my initials on it. Oh, I'm thankful, I hated losing it, and I'm relieved that's all he wanted.

I mumble, 'Thank you,' and snatch the pen. Then I step up on to the cart. I know he is still watching me.

My face is burning. As the cart rumbles out of the yard and out on to the road, I look up the other way. There is the little window, high up, in the room at the top of the spiral stairs. There's no candlelight flickering there, but then it's daytime.

They don't want to know me anyway. So I turn away.

We trundle down the road that leads to the rest of the world. Beth is right. Mr Silk is just an eccentric who likes to show off, that's all. He is a nerd about the nineteenth century, and he seeks attention from everybody, like a spoiled child.

I look down at the gold pen in my hand. Where did he find it? I look closer. Bound round it tightly is golden hair.

PART THREE

Don't turn away

ABOVE BLACK WATER GLEAMS THE BUILDING.
AT THE TOP THERE IS A WINDOW.
TWO FACES WATCH FROM THAT SMALL WINDOW,
WATCH THE CART SET OUT BACK TO THE WORLD.

15

'Not again, Daniel'

'Skiing in Switzerland under frosty blue skies! Think of that, Daniel.'

Mr Silk's voice is fat with smugness.

'Now the first historical adventure holiday is over, we can relax. It was a complete success, Daniel,' he says. 'Well done, all of us. Tell me, where is our little girl, our Sally?'

'She's in her room,' I mutter. 'She's drawing pictures of the horse and cart. We saw them leave.'

'Then I will let you tell her the news, Danny boy! Switzerland awaits. The Alps anticipate. Oh, not *you*, of course. I plan a week's skiing. What a treat!'

'When will you go, Mr Silk?' I must sound calm. I mustn't give anything away.

'Oh, early January perhaps. Or February. Don't worry, I'll make some kind of provision for you both. In fact, my wife may not accompany me . . .'

January. I thought he meant tomorrow or next week!

I can't wait until January. Certainly not until February. If Mrs Silk does go with him, then who . . . he won't bring anyone from outside to look after us. He'll just leave us more food . . . All these long dreary years suddenly seem like nothing! Now that I've made the promise, I want to leave. I want to run from the mill, run away anywhere.

I tell Sally that Mr Silk plans to go to Switzerland.

'Switzerland?' she echoes. 'Where Heidi was, with her grandpa and the goats?'

'That's right, Sally. Think of the Silks on their skis, Sally! His legs are too long and thin and hers too short and fat.' I snort with laughter and throw myself to the floor waving my arms and legs. 'Oh dear, Emmanuel Silk has whooshed straight into a very deep snowdrift. He can't get out! And his fat missus has been buried by an avalanche!' I crow.

She forces a little smile. She can't take much more.

She says, 'Why didn't we run off with Rachel? She would know the way.'

'Because, Sally, no one is safe. Not for us. We can't trust anyone. Rachel would send us back here.'

I dream every night now. This night I dream of eggs. I dream about a big, white egg. It falls from our window and smashes on the stone. It cracks, all over the top. Stuff comes out. Then the top of the egg is in the water, just underneath, glimmering white. It breaks the surface, and it is Mr Silk's face tight inside the egg under his smashed skull. His eyes are pale, they have no pupils. He's dead! But he is alive too, because he grins.

I sit up, full of dread, drenched in sweat.

Winter comes early. It wraps its arms tight round the mill and squeezes. The sky hangs with billows of snow-cloud, as if they are curtains round a four-poster bed.

'Look, the world is covered with icing sugar,' cries Sally in the early morning, and claps her hands. She loves snow at first, until our room grows icy cold.

Later we tear at cabbage in the frosted garden. Sally's hair glows in the drabness. Years ago when we were small, Mrs Silk gave Sally a packet of seeds. Sally filled small pockets in the wall with earth. She pushed the seeds in and, months later, red and orange nasturtiums spilled down the dark stone.

Today Mr Silk is here in the garden.

He's still as a statue. A stone body in a sarcophagus.

He has that particular look in his eyes. How many times have I seen it? A detachment, as if his spirit has left him. He watches Sally as she tries to hack open the hard earth with her trowel. She hums away to herself. Sometimes a tame robin appears on long legs, his eyes bright as elderberries, and seems to listen to her.

She sings, '*The North Wind doth blow, and we shall have snow, and what will the robin do then, poor –*' She stops.

She knows he's there.

He speaks. Low and cold. Soon I will be big enough to –

'Daniel. Go up to your room,' he says.

Full of foreboding, I go up those stairs and lie on my bed with a pillow over my head. I don't want to hear.

I fall into dreamless sleep, as opaque as the millpond. When I wake I creep down the stairs to look for her.

At the bottom of the stairs lies a bundle of rags.

What is left of her hair is wet with sweat. She cannot speak.

I fetch water in a cup and wash her arms, and what parts of her damaged body she will let me see. After a while she whispers something. I put my ear near to her lips. After an age she whimpers, 'Not again, Daniel. Not again.'

I sit by her. I say, 'Tell me when you can move, Sally. Without hurting too much.' When at last she inclines her head, I put my arm round her and the other hand under her elbow and we inch our way upstairs.

He does not come near us again that day. A tray is left at the bottom of the stairs with soup (thicker than usual), bread and cheese, dark fruit cake and orange juice.

Mr Silk is sated. He does not need to see us.

He won't come near us for a few days now, I'm sure. He is bloated with his cruelty.

But I keep hearing Sally's small voice: 'Not again, Daniel. Not again.'

I know this time is a dreadful warning. It has never been so bad.

He won't go *back* again. He won't hurt her less next time, and there will be a next time, I know that for sure. He does it again and again. The more he hurts her, the more he wants to hurt her. Next time –

Steady yourself, Daniel. I take a sheet from my bed and methodically tear it into strips to bind round our feet. That's what the apprentices did in the old days to keep their feet from cold. You want us to be mill children, Mr Silk? And so we will.

That night I see his car inch out along the snow-dusted road. It's a black car, sleek and shiny, and I think it cost a great deal of money.

'It befits me, Daniel,' he boasted to me when he bought it. 'It is an appropriate vehicle for a gentleman of my standing.'

I pray that the Silks will be gone for hours on some occasion, a concert or a dinner dance. The Silk-wife loves these dinner dances. In my imagination she twirls like a spinning top under Silk's long arm. He smiles down at her. She is desperate to please him, but she never quite manages it. Once I saw her smiling up at him, with colour on her face, a fine white collar of lace, like the stars of elderflower, and her hair loose about her shoulders, like a girl's. He did not even notice. Her smile faded at last.

I think he despises her.

'Put on all the clothes you have, Sally,' I tell her, and she's too weak to argue.

I pack the bread, cheese and fruit cake, take the candle and we pick our way downstairs and past the hunchbacked shapes crouched there. He hasn't bothered to lock the outside door. Why should he fear our escape tonight when he has left Sally broken as a doll?

I hold the candle high and grip her arm tight as we stand outside.

There is the deep pond, dark as jet.

'Goodbye, little bird!' whispers Sally. 'Sleep safe in your nest in the reeds. We won't see you again. Must we go up the dale, Daniel?'

'Yes. If we go down along the road to the rest of the world, he may see us in the headlights if he returns soon. We must go the other way.'

The snowflakes spin like spangles from a mirrorball. We slither round the black pond with Sally clinging to my arm, and take the path along the greedy river.

'It's too dark!' I can hear her teeth chattering.

'Later I'll make a brand from sticks and reeds,' I promise. 'I've got the matches. But I dare not light it yet.'

'Wait!' says Sally.

We turn. Back down the valley we see the mill jutting out like a prison hulk, above the black pool and the white froth of the race. Suddenly it is all lit with silver! The moon slides out from behind the snow-clouds and its silver light spells the mill unreal. If only it *were*.

'Is that where we live, Daniel?' asks Sally.

My heart lifts. 'No, Sally! It's where we *used* to live. Come on.'

16

Sally has gone

The higher we climb, the thicker the snow falls.

I can hear her trying to push down the sob that rises in her throat. I don't blame her. The cold wind cuts us like a scythe, but we won't give in to weakness.

'Come on, Sally, come on! There it is now: shelter!'

Ahead of us is a dark mass.

She's hanging back, I have to pull her by the arm.

'That is the mouth of Hell,' she cries.

'Don't be stupid, girl,' I shout and I drag her into the darkness.

It's quieter in the cave, blessed quiet. We huddle on the floor.

'The snow is like bandages,' I tell her. 'It's going to make Egyptian mummies out of us and lay us in the rock!'

She doesn't laugh. She just pulls a sour little face and tells me to make a fire.

I gather a few sticks and twigs and old leaves and take out the matches. At last a weak flame flutters in the little heap. We nibble the oatcakes for tea and then sleep, broken by the winds that moan hungrily around the cave mouth.

I think morning comes at last but it is such a dim world, I cannot really tell if the sun ever rose or not. We struggle to stand up and I see Sally set her lips tight together. How brave she is! I don't tell her of her courage because it's better not to speak at all. We need every bit of energy we can get.

We start up the dale again. Buttresses of limestone hang over our heads, luminescent as ghostly galleons. The sky is gravid with snow. The closed dale throws back the rush of the river, the echoes of waterbirds and owls confused by the gloom.

And then I hear something scuttering beneath tree roots.

'Shh!' I whisper, finger to my lips.

I pause, then pounce, and snatch the rabbit by its long legs. It screams! I didn't know it would scream like that; pitiful, piercing cries. I drop it, and it runs off. It is so very little. But it would have been so tender.

'Good!' says Sally firmly. 'I don't want you to kill a bunny, Daniel!'

'So what are we going to eat, stupid?' I shout at her but she ignores me like she does when she isn't going to give in and says,

'Look, Daniel, I think we go that way.'

She points through the snow to the other side of the dale.

'No, not that way, Sally. Trust me.' She pulls a face and then she finds a few hazelnuts left on the bushes. They are blackened by cold.

'I'd much rather have rabbit, cooked tender on a fire!' I snap. 'I can't eat those.'

Neither can Sally. And neither can we face the withered elderberries or the watercress dying in the river. Once it was the poor man's bread. Now it is dying, brown and slimy.

'We should have waited until spring,' I say. 'Then we could go to London and I could get work. I would find something, somehow.'

'No. I couldn't stand it any longer, Daniel. I would go on my own if you wouldn't come.'

'Oh really! You wouldn't get far without *me*.'

She looks at me, defiantly. I see a different Sally out here, in this world of snow.

I feel weak and cold and starving hungry and the river is so full of tumbling water . . . of course! Fish! Why didn't I think of fish!

I slither down the bank, grasping at curtains of black ivy. Little spangles of ice shatter in the mud. I crouch in the river and at last I catch a fish that slips and twists in my hands.

The fish cooks crisp and black, too black, but inside the flesh is soft and white.

'Mind the bones, Daniel,' she warns me, licking her fingers. We feel better after that fish.

On we go again. The dale is growing narrower, a weal never open to the light. The frost glistens without melting. All day the dark waits for us in the hollows, and in the late afternoon it creeps out once more across the pock-marked snow. And then Sally starts to cry. 'Stop it!' I hiss at her, but she can't. Then she is sick. I know our feet are swollen and bleeding raw under the rags.

'Let's sit awhile, Sally,' I say and we sink down on to the snow, our backs resting against a log. We watch our breath in the damp air.

'We're breathing dragon smoke,' she says. She's never low for long. 'My feet hurt, Daniel. I want to take the rags off.'

'No! You'll never get your boots back on again. Just rest, Sally, please!'

She turns her face away from me, up to the white sky. And then the sun comes out. It lights up the ridge in the west and gilds the dale as if it had a brushful of gold.

'I want to go to the sun!' she shouts and points. 'Up there, Danny. Look!'

'No. Don't be so stupid, Sally! I know which way to go. We're safe down here, we're hidden. If we go up to the top of the ridge in the sunlight we will be seen for miles!'

But she keeps looking at me, her blue eyes full of pleading. I can't stand it.

'I want the sun, Danny,' she insists. Sally can be so stubborn sometimes! But I am not going to listen to her.

And suddenly she is up on her feet and away, skipping down the dale and across the little stream and up the other side. She scrambles towards that golden edge, pulling herself up by rocks and roots, setting off little hailstorms of scree that tumble down after her.

She's gone. Sally has gone.

17
Danny the odd one out

'She'll be back in a minute,' I say to myself. 'She can't stand being without me.'

I peel slivers of damp bark from the log and wait. I imagine Sally standing in the sunshine for a while craving its warmth and then scampering back to me when the shadows creep towards her.

I stand up and have a good stretch. I'm not going to hurry after her, I'm tired and hungry. I amble across to the other side of the dale, thinking of Sally at the top, her face loving the sunlight and in spite of my anger at her, silly girl, I just have to smile. She would sing 'In the Bleak Midwinter'. She likes that one, that and 'The North Wind doth blow'.

'All right, Sally,' I say grudgingly, 'it is cheering in this sunlight. Not that the winter sun makes much difference for long. It's a false promise. It's weak and it hardly warms me at all.'

I shiver again and know that the sun is fading fast.

In winter the darkness is with you all day. It creeps up behind you without a sound, but stops when you turn to catch it, as if you're playing What's the time, Mr Wolf? Once you turn your back on it again, it spreads like an inky cloud of disguise.

I slither down the other side of the ridge on to a road. The surface is black and shiny from the melted snow. Sally must have trotted along this road. She'll be singing 'Little Donkey' by now. And she'll be seen! And she mustn't go back near the river on her own; she'll drown.

'Which way? *Which way*?'

The way that seems to go nearer to the sun, of course. Sally thinks she can reach the sun. When we see rainbows from our window, Sally always thinks you can run to the end and find the pot of gold.

I hurry along the road, listening for her singing or her footsteps. Without Sally, I tell you, the silence begins to squeeze at my chest.

What will she do? She'll be lost. She has no maps in her head. It's hard for her even to find her way around the mill. She can't read properly and she could not see well. Cold as I am, I feel the sweat of fear break out on my neck.

I must cover as much ground as possible. I keep near the road, though not on it.

I hide as a black car slides past. When I can no longer

hear the engine I turn and retrace my steps for a mile or so, but there's no Sally. I settle in a hollow for the night. I dream stupidly of the Owl and the Pussycat and bread and honey and lots of money.

And now, this morning, the snow stops. Mist swirls in and out of the hills like a long scarf, hiding summits and then suddenly revealing them like a magic trick. I hurry on, careful to keep just below the ridge, trying to stop the pictures storming through my mind: Sally calling my name; Sally running down the road before a big black car; Silk's elbow resting on the window; Sally's small body on the snow, her golden fan of hair spread around her face.

At the end of a track stands a milk churn. I make a cup of my hands and drink. It's so rich! I cup my hands again and then stop to listen.

From a nearby barn come voices, mumbling, low and in a rhythm. I tiptoe to the door and peer in. Figures crouch on stools. Whether they are men or women I cannot tell. Their heads are bound in cloth and their chins on their chests as they milk the cows and chant.

Prayers? If they are, then they are prayers I cannot understand. They might be in a foreign tongue, they might be calling up the Devil himself.

I run, fast, away through a wood.

Something twitches in the corner of my eye. A tree. It's moving! The tree is full of ragged birds. I believe they are birds of ill omen. They flap and rustle thickly among the branches. One stretches a ragged wing on the wind. It tears. I rub my tired eyes and look again. They aren't birds at all, but black plastic from the bales of cut grass in the fields.

And then I come to a halt! There's a fence, and I'm at the edge of the wood, and I can see a spread of buildings stretching below me. The sky is full of the peal of bells! The noise shocks me. Round the church tower wheel clouds of birds, mesmerised by the ringing. There's a background hum of engines.

I stop dead. Lots of heads are watching me. They are all behind a big window, in boxes. They are all the same head. They turn suddenly and look past me. They vanish. In their place are cars, the same car.

Mrs Silk had one of those boxes in her sitting-room. A television. Sally and I would peep through the window, and Mr Silk roared in rage if he discovered us. His wife spent a lot of time staring at it. This shop sells them. The big window with the flickering pictures makes me shake my head fast, makes my eyes feel fixed as if they are pulled out on rods.

Sally must be somewhere in this busy town. She will love it. I tell you, and I wouldn't tell Sally, it terrifies me. I unwind the rags on my feet and leave them under a tree. I hurry along the road and into a market. Garments of pink and blue and black hang above stalls, glossy books and packets of sweets and biscuits are set out in rows.

There's a stall covered with emerald green grass. It's too shiny to be real. There are apples and oranges built up into pyramids, so many different shapes and colours. The heady smell of the fruit makes me feel drunk. I feel as if I'm assaulted, bashed about by so many things, so many people, so much noise. I keep my head down. I remember the big snow-dappled horse wears cups by his eyes, blinkers I think they are called. I'd like some.

There's a stall that sells shoes, hundreds of pairs, in and out of boxes, slippers in tartan and red, shiny black witch's shoes with needle heels, rubber boots, laced leather boots for giants, snow-white shoes labelled 'trainers'. Which shoes to choose? Boots? None of them look warm. And in this town it's warmer, a topcoat warmer than the dale.

I step back to watch a group of lads swagger past. They wear shiny wide-backed jackets and trousers of dark blue cotton and walk easy on spongy shoes with big soles like the ones on the stall. I want to shrink and vanish as they amble past. They *know*, don't they? They know I'm a misfit, know I don't belong here, know I have lost Sally. *Danny the odd one out* . . .

Round the other side of the stall a woman in a brown apron with wide pockets busies herself finding boots for an old lady. I help myself to some shoes like the boys wore and put them under my jacket.

I saunter towards a little brick house marked Toilets.

They don't smell quite as bad as the latrine at the mill, and there is soap. The shoes are a little too big, like white boats, but that is as well because my feet are rubbed raw. How light these trainers are, springy after the clogs or boots we've always had to wear! I dump my old boots in a wire basket with lots of paper and soggy food, then I walk out along the busy street, turning my head from side to side, careful not to meet anyone's eye, my heart pounding and grown bigger under my ribs.

And then I see it.

A magic house in a bow-fronted shop window. A notice says *Gingerbread Cottage*. It is cinnamon-dark, with window-panes of chocolate blocks and iced tiles on the roof. It has barley sugar chimneys. My eyes fill with tears as I think how Sally would love it, the little garden with marzipan tulips and a lawn of green icing.

My mouth waters, I'm sure I can smell its rich sweetness through the window. And Sally would be trying to see the witch through the little windows. She would walk her fingers up the path of sugar crystals, and pick the icing flowers to nibble with her little almond teeth.

Two flat biscuit figures lean against the gingerbread house. They have icing eyes and buttons and smiling mouths. One of them has squiggles of yellow icing for her hair.

'I know who you are,' I tell them. 'You're the Gingerbread Man. And his girl. One for each of us, Sally.'

'Can I help you?'

She stands in the shop doorway. She's as tall as I am, and she's very pretty, with curls like the gingerbread girl. Her skin has the softness of a peach, the sheen of good health, food and sunlight.

'I'm looking at the gingerbread men,' I say.

'They're fifty pence each.'

I know my eyes will work on her and do the trick. I can soften this girl up like lard in sunshine.

'I've come out without my money,' I say and give a little shrug, a wan smile.

She glances over her shoulder into the shop.

'Wait,' she whispers. She goes inside and comes out again, and passes a bag into my hand. 'See you!' she calls.

I hurry down the road and round the corner. There I stop. I can't wait. I untie the pink squirly ribbon on the cellophane and take out the biscuit man. I bite off his head.

'Is that nice, Daniel?'

The hand on my shoulder presses hard until it hurts. Those long fingers dig right in.

'You're such a kind boy! You're saving the gingerbread girl for Sally, aren't you?' says Mr Silk. 'She'll enjoy it. She's waiting for you, Daniel.'

PART FOUR

Out into the light

18

One step at a time

'Rachel? *Rachel*! What on earth are these?'

Sam flicks them as if he's shuffling playing cards. 'I just found them on my desk.'

'Oh, they're postcards from that awful mill. I brought them back with me. I never got round to getting stamps. Or posting them.'

He turns each card and skim-reads the back. I wait. I was on my way to the kitchen to make a cup of tea but now I can't move. Those few days pour over me and I'm set in cement.

'Thanks for the axolotls,' he says. 'But are you sure you went to the right place? Sounds like teenage girls' imaginings to me. Spooks and poltergeists and villains in the night?'

'Don't be patronising, Sam!' I really don't want to think about the mill. I've been trying to keep it out of my mind. I take in a great deep breath to crack the cement but it doesn't work. 'Sam, don't scoff. Please.' Because I think I will cry if you do. 'There *was* something strange happening, but no one else seemed to notice. The whole thing was weird anyway! We had to play at being cotton apprentices, dressing up and writing on slates and stuff. But there were two others. I think they were there all the time. It wasn't pretending for them. They weren't playing. They really lived like that. I think.'

'You think! How do you mean?'

'They had no electricity in their rooms. They wore old-fashioned clothes.'

'Probably very good for them!' said Sam. 'No telly, no junk food, no consumer society. Come on, Rache, a lot of people are nostalgic for the past. Maybe this was just an extra bit of show. What's this about someone getting hurt?'

'*Nobody*. I mean, I didn't actually see anyone hurt . . . I just sensed something. The whole thing was like, sometimes I saw clearly, sometimes I lost it. The man at the mill, the Director man. We had to call him the Master! He had this girl and boy living there. I don't know if he fostered them, or what. They wouldn't say much. Especially the boy. They were so – apart.'

'Did this Director man have a wife?'

'Yes. But she didn't have much to do with them. Honestly, Sam, sometimes I'm not even sure they were *there* . . . It's like they were ghosts.'

'Come on, Rachel, you know there are no ghosts!'

I don't. Not since I stayed at Narrow Dale Mill. I don't know what I believe any more. I don't want to think about it. I don't want anything that's not easy, not nice, not black and white. I want life to smooth out now. I want a straight and shining path with no twists and turns and no shadows. I get up in the morning, eat my toast and Marmite, go to school and it's good. Dad's back at work, trying to make up for lost time. It's Sam's first year at medical school. The college is in Nottingham so he can live at home, and it's easy and of course it's cheaper. He's out most of the time working hard. That's what he tells us, anyway. We're a functioning family. We eat and sleep and work and go to the supermarket three times a week and put our clothes in the washing-machine and open tins of smelly dog stuff for Wally and bath him in rosemary dog shampoo. He still smells.

I still see Nikki and Gemma a bit, but not so much. Helen Anderson changed schools. I think I know why.

I'm working hard now. I feel driven. I like it. They're surprised at school. Miss Benson almost smiles if she sees me in the corridor. Once she called out, 'You're winning, Rachel!' But I know I'm only picking my way, one step at a time on fragile ice . . .

And it's that time of year, the darkness of short days closing in like book-ends. The back end of the year, they call it. I don't like it. Yesterday on the way to the bus I saw a gang of those ragged black birds; you know, the big ones with the voices flat as saws. They were shambling into the road to mob a dead cat. One stretched out a tatty wing and I had a glimpse of sheen on the dim black. Then it dulled.

'Rachel,' says Sam now, 'I think you're worrying over something that isn't there. You've let your imagination run away with you.'

Perhaps he's right. I look for drama where there is none.

That night it takes me ages to fall asleep. I keep getting up and looking out at the moon. The moon is full. A cloud scuds across and makes the moon blink.

There is a face in the moon, I've always thought that. Can't remember if the face is supposed to be made of *cream* cheese or *green* cheese . . . or does it eat cheese? Or . . . I'm very sleepy.

'Rachel? RACHEL!'

I've slept late. I totter downstairs with my duvet round me like a chrysalis, I'll watch Saturday morning telly from the sofa like a little kid. I'll eat my Shreddies from a bowl. I'll . . .

'Rachel. Did you really *have* to?'

'Have to *what*?'

'Did you have to send another postcard? And without a stamp too? I had to pay!'

I peer at the card he's flapping in front of me. What a

state it's in, all muddy and sort of wilted, as if it's got wet. The address is in my writing.

'And what's this? A child's drawing?'

It did look as if a child had drawn it. They were good drawings. There was a castle with turrets. A round face smiled over the battlements. The face was framed by a mass of hair, like the petals on a chrysanthemum.

Sally.

19

'Is there anybody there?'

'Rachel? *Rachel*! What's the matter with you today?'

It's my dear big brother roaring from the bathroom. He'll feature a lot this weekend, I know, because Dad isn't back until tomorrow night.

'What do you mean, Sam?' I sing out, so sweet and innocent.

'The phone! It's been ringing and ringing. Why didn't you answer it? I can't go right now!'

'Phone? I didn't hear it, actually, Sam. I was getting dressed.'

To tell the truth I'm dazed. I've been thinking, why did Sally send me that card? Where did she post it? And then I've been picturing Daniel. Was she with him when she posted the card? Did he ask about me, say my name, make a note of my number? Mr Fit. Mr Gorgeous. Mr Divinely Deliciously Demonic. Mr . . .

'*RACHEL!*'

And this time I hear it, the persistent, shrill ringing, and I throw myself down the stairs and burst into the sitting-room, trampling over Wally, and grabbing the receiver so that the phone falls off the windowledge and dangles from the cord.

I crouch and shout into the receiver, 'Hello?'

Beep beep beep. It's a payphone. They can't get their money in. They haven't got the right change perhaps. Haven't they heard of phone cards? I feel smug. I have a phone card! Not that it was any use at the mill, because there wasn't a public telephone.

'Is there anybody there?' I shout, hold the receiver at arm's length and look at it.

Wally looks at me from the other side of the room. How dare I disturb his sleep.

The phone has long since stopped beeping. It burrs instead. I replace it carefully.

'Must be one of your penniless mates, Sam,' I bawl. 'Or your fancy woman.' Not that he'd tell me if he had one.

Then I have a sudden conviction. The phone call. It's *them*. It's Sally and Daniel. Don't ask me why I think that. Today I'm trusting my instinct. Today I'm listening to *myself*.

Sally can't still be at the mill if she sent the card. But if she sent the card, she wouldn't have my phone number any more.

Daniel could have remembered it. He could cope with numbers, Sally said.

There's the phone again. I snatch it up.

'Rachel!' says Dad's voice. 'How are you?'

Oh. 'Fine,' I mutter.

'Are you sure, love?'

'Yes, Dad.' It's not his fault I'm disappointed. I'd just hoped to hear Daniel's gravelly voice saying my name.

'How's Sam?' asks Dad brightly.

'He's in the bathroom with the door locked. He's fine too.'

'Oh. Good. Well, I'll be back tomorrow evening, about seven I hope. As long as you're both fine. Done your homework?'

He always asks that, he's so predictable. 'Of course I've done it, Dad! Why couldn't you get through before?'

'Eh?'

'When you rang before. You couldn't get through.'

'But this is the first time I've rung. I suppose you two have just got up, Rachel.'

My mind is racing.

'Rachel? I'll see you tomorrow. Maybe we'll get a take-away. Rachel?'

He sounds puzzled, hurt even. He's miffed because I'm not really interested in him just now.

I say quickly, 'Great. Let's have a curry. You can tell us all about your weekend.'

'It's about environmentally beneficial waste disposal. Recycling nappies. Cesspits. Friendly fertilisers. That kind of thing.'

'Ah. Wow, Dad. Great. Well. I look forward to seeing you anyway. Bye, Dad.'

I wait anxiously for the phone to ring again. It doesn't. By the time Sam ambles into the room all squeaky clean, my mind is made up.

'We have to do some shopping today, Sam. I have to go to Jessops for – er – more tights and another school blouse.' He frowns. 'And we need to do a food shop,' I tell him. 'It'll take the weight off Dad next week if we do the big shop today.'

'We?'

'Yes. Come on, I can't carry it all! Anyway, Dad doesn't like me going round the city centre on my own.'

'First time it's ever bothered you.' He sighs, a long-suffering sigh. 'All right,' he says. 'I'll take you if it'll shut you up.'

So out we go to Sam's little black car. He has a special blanket on the back seat for hairy Wally to travel neatly, but Wally always tries to squirm on to my knee in front. Today Wally can't come. Not to Jessop's.

'By the way,' I say nonchalantly. 'Can we have a quick look at the castle? I haven't been there for years.'

20

'What will you do without her, Daniel?'

Mrs Silk has been here.

She has arranged Sally's room. On Sally's pillow lies the second-best doll, the scrubbing brush doll. I used to call it Hedgehog and Sally was cross. Next to Hedgehog, a family of peg dolls are lined up. Sally didn't have time to do that before we left.

I cross to the window and look down. Sure enough, like a little ferry, the bird steams out from the rushes on to the still waters. Is it the same bird? It paddles its tranquil circles, unaware of the turbulence so near.

Here the world is hushed by snow. Yet into this silence moves the sound of water, quiet at first, then growing. The angry river. I put my hands to my head and feel my skull holding back a mill race, a rage ready to burst.

When he first brought me back, he leaned in the doorway and watched me as I ran into the room calling her name.

'Oh dear, Daniel. Can't you find her?' He is unreal with his exaggerated gestures. He thinks he is on a stage, playing the Master of Mockery.

'Where *is* she? What have you done with her?'

'I was hoping you might tell me that, Daniel. I knew you'd come back easily if you thought Sally was here. She isn't. What will you do without her, Daniel? You're like Siamese twins.'

The room is dim. The candles are unlit. Nothing gives light.

'Tell me where she is, Daniel.' His soft voice has a blade of threat in it, buried deep down.

'I don't know, I don't know! She ran off. She could be anywhere!'

'She won't be far away,' says Silk. 'She'll come back here to you, Daniel. You are all she knows, this room is her home, after all these years.'

'*But why?* Why do you keep us here? We're prisoners. Why are we here?'

Mr Silk smiles. He lifts his shoulders in a shrug as if he's quite, quite helpless.

'Because you are here,' he says. 'Because that's your life, Daniel. You couldn't live any other way now, could you? I have brought you up in the way I think fit. Fit for all of us. That is my right, isn't it? As parent or guardian? It's a question of individual freedom, Daniel.'

I hear the bolts slam on the outside of the door and his footsteps on the stairs.

It goes on like that. He comes and leans there and watches and talks at me. Sometimes he hurts me. I am too weak to put up a fight. I won't always be weak.

I bide my time, resting with my back against the wall, while I feel as if he's pulled my heart from my chest and is squeezing it slowly in his long hands.

I wrap my arms round my knees and rest my head on them. All I want is to see the brightness of her hair, my beacon in the dark.

I remember Mr Silk putting the patch cap on that hair, more than once. First he shaved her head. He put the cut hair in a paper bag. I don't know what he did with it. Then he smeared on black tarry stuff, then the rubber cap, to kill head-lice. That's what they used to do to the apprentices in the old days, said Mr Silk. He did it to me too. Hours later he dragged it off again. The cap pulled our hair out by the roots. I bit my mouth so that I didn't cry out. Sally screamed and screamed. I made vows to myself then, vows of what I would do to him. I didn't tell them to Sally, I didn't dare.

But we didn't have head-lice.

We searched for them in each other's hair, like terrified monkeys and we never found one!

'My dear children, *all* apprentices have head-lice,' cried Mr Silk. 'Lice are as pearly grey as beads of barley, with scrambly legs and mouths that bite and make you scratch red raw.'

Our heads bled and we looked ridiculous, but at least we were together.

I can't stand these days alone. It's so dark, the world is in a coma. Short, dark, dying days. And then I remember about Advent. The Second Coming. Arrival. The time of Judgement. Change. End and beginning. I fasten these words up at the backs of my eyelids and read them again and again to keep myself alive.

There's a stub of candle in a tin on the floor near me. The tallow has melted into white worm casts in the tin. The candle has burned a sooty cloud on the wall behind it. I pull the matches from my pocket and light it. I look at the glow and half close my eyes, making the light split into a burst of little yellow rays. It cannot last long, but it is a comfort! The candle is a tiny lighthouse beaming golden strands. I think of Sally's hair, like marigold petals on her white neck, and if she's not here, then Silk can't hurt her.

It's just as well she's gone.

21

Maybe it was all a game

My big brother is sulking! He stomps ahead, hands in his pockets.

'Come on, Sam! We can have an ice-cream!'

'Not in November,' he grumbles.

Nottingham Castle doesn't really look like a castle at all. We came here when I was little and I told Mum she had brought us to the wrong place. It isn't a pretty fairytale castle with towers and turrets and maidens in wimples. The old castle was destroyed and this one was built in its place. It looks like a public library or a bank.

'It's too cold to sightsee,' moans my brother. 'It's ages since we've been up there. Why do you want to go? It's something to do with the apprentice kids, isn't it? But you don't know anything for certain, Rache.'

That's Sam. That's my brother, everything has to be *for certain*. Scientific. Proven. He won't go on his instinct.

Perhaps he doesn't have any instinct.

'Oh come on, Sam, a walk will do you good. The weather's not too bad now and the shopping's done. I just fancy a walk up there.'

'You're the only one who does, then,' he grumbles, turning up his collar. 'We haven't passed a living soul.'

Everything round here has names connected with Robin Hood: Maid Marian's Tea Rooms, Friar Tuck Tavern, Merry Men Pizzeria. Sam says there was no such bimbo as Maid Marian. Robin Hood and his mates in green were renegades, terrorists, outlaws. Now they sell burgers and doughnuts, Little John lemonade and Sherwood milkshakes.

Now it seems that Daniel and Sally are runaways too, living outside everything.

The cold wind makes my eyes stream. I'm looking for two figures, everywhere. Sam's right, everyone has stayed inside this cold day. No one wants to be a tourist struggling up the hill against the wind.

I like this space in the middle of the city, the grass and the trees and the hulk of the castle up on the rock; it's a kind of freedom. I can see why they built castles. You could look down on the busy city, you could remember that hills and countryside are part of the world, but get back quick to your castle which sails the hillside like a galleon. And you could see your enemies coming. You would know at once who they were.

The old moat has been drained to make a path through banks thick with butterbur and ivy. Most of the snow has melted here in the city and the castle remains in the scent of wet earth, as if it has been left behind.

We mooch around, heads down, hands in pockets. I'm *freezing*, but I daren't say anything or Sam will do his I-told-you-so-Rachel routine.

'Let's walk nearer the wall. It's more sheltered,' he says, and we hurry across and follow the path by the wall. Monsters sit on the walls, monsters of stone; griffins and crossbreed dragons, watching over us.

We hurry into the castle to get warm. There are few visitors today. We glance at arty painted pots and vases, different costumes, jewellery and the white froth of Nottingham lace.

My eyes are everywhere, my heart floating high, hoping to see Daniel. Why didn't *he* write on the card? I know he can read and write because Sally told me.

'Come on, I've had enough,' says Sam 'and the chips will de-frost before we get home.'

All right, my instinct was wrong, they're not here, they're still in that high dark room at the mill. Maybe it was all a game they played on me? Some strange game between the two of them? Maybe they're warm and laughing in Mr Silk's sitting-room with a bag of salt and vinegar crisps and *Top of the Pops*.

We trudge back along the terrace paths and I wonder what to do now. I can't ignore the way I feel. Should I go to the police? They'll think I'm off my trolley. I haven't got any real facts about anything. I –

'Blimey, they get younger and younger,' says my brother. Sometimes he sounds about ninety.

'Who do?'

'The down and outs. The tramps. Look at that one over there. In the hollow.'

I stare at the huddle of clothes in the recess of the stone wall. I can see the white of a face wrapped round with grey cloth, but there are tendrils of hair, bright as nasturtium flowers.

'Sally!'

She stumbles to her feet and cries, 'You've been a long time, Rachel.'

I put my arms round her and she presses her wet face on to my shoulder.

So many questions bubble in my brain, but the first one is, 'Where's Daniel?'

'Dunno.'

'Is he still at the mill?'

'He said he was going to a city,' she says. 'To London. Like Dick Whittington. He's clever, Daniel, he could get a job, could Daniel. He could look after me.'

'Why isn't he still with you, Sally?'

'I lost him. I wanted to go the other way. And then I was cross with him because he wouldn't go where I wanted and I ran off and then I couldn't see him any more.'

She looks up at me, her eyes swimming with tears. 'I'm no good at left and right. I can't find the way.'

'But you've done really well, Sally! How long have you been here?'

'One dark night. No, two, I think. Dunno,' she whispers.

Sally glances sideways at Sam. I can see she's frightened of him, of everything.

Sam smiles his disarming smile and tells her, 'I'm Rachel's brother, but she's too rude to introduce me.'

He glances down at her feet all wrapped in filthy rags and the smile vanishes. The more he looks, the harder he frowns and I want to laugh. How will he cope with someone like Sally? She will have his neat little world in tatters!

And then I catch my breath because the thought of her anywhere near a road is terrifying! What about rivers and canals? Could she swim if she fell in? She's not safe alone.

'How did you get all the way to Nottingham, Sally?' I ask.

'Oh. Well, when I couldn't find Daniel I went down the road. And I got to a village. And then this car was in the road and it nearly squashed me down. She was sorry, the woman. She said, "Where are you going, duck?" So I said, "Nottingham Castle." "Are you sure, duck?" "Yes please." And I got in the car. It was nice and purry. It was warm. She bought me a sandwich, Rachel. At a garage place. For petrol. It smelled. Then when we got to all the red houses. She said, "This is Nottingham. Get out now." '

'Sally, you really mustn't trust people like that. You don't just get in people's cars!'

'But she was a kind woman, Rachel! She was sorry that she nearly knocked me down.' She smiled and I saw Sam smile back. Anyone's heart would be melted by that smile.

Sally says, 'The woman kept going, "Pooh!" and doing this,' and she waves her hand under her nose. 'She said to me, "You could use a bath, duck." '

The woman was dead right, but Sam's had all the hot water. I'll put on the immersion heater the second we get back.

'Why did you come to the castle, Sally? Why didn't you ask the woman to bring you to my house? I gave you my address.'

'Didn't have your house any more. The woman saw me looking at it, and she said, "There's a postbox down the road. There was a red thing with a mouth. I put the postcard in the mouth and it fell. She was fed up with me. She said she had lots to do and she didn't want to get into anything. I don't know what she meant.' Sally tilts her head on one side and says, 'I did thank her, Rachel!'

'I'm sure you did. She was a kind woman, and you

were very very lucky. But you mustn't be friendly with strangers, Sally.'

'Don't tell Daniel,' she whispers.

'I won't,' I promise, thinking, if we ever see him again.

'Sally, did you phone my house? I suppose you couldn't if my number was on the postcard.'

She pushes up her sleeve. On her grimy skin was my telephone number, written in blue pen. 'I could press the numbers, but then it kept making a funny noise and I didn't know what to do. And I didn't have any money.'

A little bud of hope began to open in me. 'Did Daniel write down my number? He'll be able to work the phone.'

'Oh I didn't tell *him* where you live,' she cries. 'Daniel will be cross if he knows I been talking to you about your number. Daniel says I mustn't. Because we will get into bad trouble if we talk to other people, more trouble than we can tell, Mrs Silk says. Mr Silk will punish Daniel. And Mr Silk, he will –' she shudders.

Deadlock, isn't it? Mr Silk plays them both off against each other.

'And now I've lost Daniel! What will he do without me?' A tear slides down her cheek.

'Come on, you two,' commands Sam. 'Let's go back to the car.' He puts his hand to Sally's elbow. She gives a little flinch, but that's all. She looks up at him and whispers,

'Daniel says I'm a changeling.'

'Oh,' says Sam. Not a lot you can say to that, really . . .

Sam leads us down through the castle gate and takes us on a little detour to see the Famous Outlaw to cheer Sally up.

'There you are, Sally! Meet Robin Hood. We only have heroes in Nottingham, you know.'

Sally trots over and gazes at the statue. This Robin Hood is carved out of bronze and built like a warrior. He looks like a Samurai with those wide shoulders and sinewy legs. Judge Dredd of the Forest.

Sam reads out the inscription: '*For he was a good outlaw, and dyde pore men moch good.* He was a right old renegade, our Robin. He'll watch over you, Sally. He'll keep you safe.'

Sally giggles. I think she believes Sam, she certainly *wants* to. So do I.

But I have this nagging feeling that Mr Silk will come looking and that he could find anybody, anywhere. Especially Sally.

Please, please let Daniel find us before Silk does.

A black car passes us and my heart jumps. I wish I had a woolly hat or something so that Sally could be disguised. I take her elbow and draw her away from the kerb, noticing as I do a spill of oil in the gutter. The brackish colours slip and slide in a greasy rainbow. I catch a gleam of violet in the slick, and then it's back to sluggish blue and brown.

'Hurry up, you two,' I hiss, wanting the safety of the car, but on the way Sam insists on buying us fresh doughnuts from a stall. Sally is in heaven, smacking her lips over their warm sweetness and licking the sugar from her fingers. She grins and I see sugar sparkling in the grime around her mouth.

Sometimes I like my brother.

22

Who am I trying to shelter?

'White musk or dewberry?'

Sally comes into the steam-filled bathroom, snug in my blue towelling robe. Her eyes widen at the torrent of hot water thundering from the tap.

'Which bath oil, Sally?'

'Oh. All of them, please!' she cries.

She drops my bath robe and climbs into the bath, scooping up bubbles and piling them on her arms. She suddenly remembers me, glances up and blushes. I try not to look at her. She must feel shy getting undressed in front of another girl. Soon she's enjoying her bath so much she forgets her shyness.

The shampoo we have is for 'normal hair' and I think, your hair is anything but normal, Sally. It's beautiful. Even if it is so uneven now.

'Wet your hair first,' I say. 'You can lie down in the water to do it.'

She slides down nervously, but the pleasure of the warm water in her hair and on her scalp is intense and then she doesn't want to sit up again. I squirt on the shampoo, I can wash other people's hair. I've washed Mum's. It didn't take long.

Sally's hair needs a lot of washing, but she likes it and we get on well. I smooth on rosemary conditioner and work it in, lots of it so we can get a brush through afterwards. She sniffs appreciatively. She shouts when I take the spray and rinse her hair.

'How do you wash your hair at the mill? Do you have a shower?'

'No. We have a bath. A tin bath. The water's not hot like this.' She splashes and shrieks and turns in the water like a porpoise and I can't help but laugh with her, she's loving it so much. Then she surfaces and says, 'Tell me about Robin Hood and his Merry Men, Rachel.'

So I tell her all I can remember about Robin of Locksley and Maid Marian, the emerald green forest, fat Friar Tuck and the Sheriff of Nottingham. I throw a couple of kings in for good measure. To tell the truth I can't remember much of the Robin Hood story except that they had arrows and wore Lincoln Green, whatever that is. Sounds like a football strip. But when I see Sally's intent face, I warm up and really get into it. I make up all sorts of details about Friar Tuck not being able to see his sandals past his tummy and Robin

Hood being the best-looking thing in the Midlands. I do the Sheriff's wicked cackle, too. Sally likes that. I have to do it again.

Suddenly I can't laugh any more. She's washed and washed, with soap, and with my loofah, scrubbing at her legs to get them clean. We've been in here for hours.

So why is the skin on her back and body still so dark?

'Sally. Erm . . . how did you get those marks on your arms and back?'

Why do I ask? I already know the answer. I know.

She hangs her head. Bath-time has been spoiled and I'm sorry.

'Did you trip on the stairs? Or fall in the yard or something?'

Who am I trying to shelter? I must be protecting someone. Is it Sally, or myself, because I don't want to think there's that kind of hurt in the world?

I wish I hadn't asked.

'It's all right, Sally,' I say. 'Get into some warm clothes. The water's getting cold.'

I look for our newest, thickest towel. She'll love it. The towel is pink with a satin trim and an embossed rose in the corner. I hold it out and she brightens up, but as I'm wrapping it round her shoulders I can't stop looking at the blue and red bruises. When I see that damage to her arms I wonder why on earth people have tattoos. And there are more marks, yellow and pale green and grey under her shiny white skin.

And she has cuts. Weals. Scratches. I don't really know what to call them. They are red and sore and one of them looks infected. I don't know what to say so I bite my lip.

'Can I go and see Wally now? Now I know he's *just a dog*,' she giggles.

(She was terrified when Wally first ambled up to her. 'It's a wolf!' she shrieked.

'No, he's just a black hearth-rug,' I said. 'It's Wally and he's just a dog.'

The poor dog was embarrassed by Sally's fear and sat in the corner gazing up at her. At last he sneaked over and she just had to touch his glossy ears.)

'You can help me feed Wally when you're dressed,' I tell her and she dashes past Sam on the landing, even though she's draped from head to foot in the pink towel.

I get out a top, pants, a sweatshirt and some jeans. She doesn't need a bra but I find a crop top with a lacy trim and she loves that.

She's very thin. The clothes hang off her but she's delighted with them. She's too hot in the sweatshirt and doesn't mind bare arms, even bare arms with bruises. She tries on some trainers too and they fit with some socks. She looks terrific!

And then, on the way towards the stairs she pushes open a door.

'No, Sally, don't! That's the wrong room . . .'

Too late.

23

I don't want to look

She hesitates in the doorway. Before I can stop her she runs into the room crying, 'Look at this beautiful coat. It's a magic coat! Is it yours, Rachel?'

The midnight coat hangs on the wardrobe door. I know it's there; Dad insists on it being there.

I don't want to look. I don't want to see it.

'Whose is this coat, Rachel?' she cries.

I have to look. She picks up a limp velvet sleeve and strokes it. She turns to smile at me.

My heart thuds, it will crack my ribs. I struggle for breath.

My voice comes out small. 'It's my mother's.'

'Where is she, Rachel?'

She watches my face. Why has she asked? Everyone knows about my mother. Don't they? Not today they don't.

'She died. My mother died.'

How strange it sounds. I don't think I've had to say it

before. Hardly anybody spoke about it. I suppose they thought I might cry and they would feel bad. Everyone knew. So I didn't have to tell them.

'What was your mother like, Rachel?'

When?

It's so hard to speak. 'She – she was smaller than me. She had brown hair and she liked gardening. She made chocolate cake. And read books. She worked some of the time. She – she was just a mum.'

Sally looks sad. 'But she died. Poor Mum. Poor Rachel. I haven't got a real mum. Was your mum a real mum, Rachel?'

'Yes.'

'I bet she was beautiful, wasn't she?'

No. Not the mother I remember. She was a pale, crumpled shape without a frame, without a structure. We had to keep shifting her, propping her up, wedging her in so that she would not fall and hurt herself. She insisted on the cushion with the silk iris always behind her neck. I see her cheek turned to it.

Her hair was thin. Her eyes weren't lovely any more. The tumour in her brain sent her eyes sliding away. Her centre was gone. And the fits she had . . . I tried not to see her. I used to make her cups of tea and help her to drink, but I never looked into her eyes. I wanted to run away to homework, school, shopping, *anything* rather than see that remnant of her slumped in the chair, like an empty paper bag.

Now Sally comforts me. She fetches a tissue from the box and dabs at my tears. Then she says, 'Who got her the magic coat, Rachel?'

'My dad. Mum fell in love with it in a shop on her birthday but it was too much money. I told Dad. He went back later and bought it for her. I'm glad he did.'

My dad. Sitting downstairs with his head in his hands.

'Did she like the coat?'

'Yes. Although she did not go out in it. She got so very ill so quickly. She wore it in the house, Sally. Dad helped her put it on and she sat in it like an empress.'

Sally strokes my hair. That makes me cry all the more. No one strokes my hair now.

It takes a while to get myself together; lots of crying and tissue-dabbing, nose-blowing and face-washing.

'Sally, I'm supposed to be looking after *you*,' I cry and then we have a little laugh.

Sam peers at my face when we go downstairs. He decides it's safer not to comment. He's poised to cook. 'You can have eggs, baked beans, mushrooms, Sally,' he says, wielding the frying pan. He's always thought frying is his job, kind of a male thing to do. Dangerous. Fine by me; I don't want my clothes to smell of fat frying.

He lists, 'Sausages, fried potatoes, onions. A burger?'

Sally dithers and giggles and really can't choose, so he does a mammoth fry-up with two pans and she goes at it full-pelt with knife, fork and fingers.

'What are we doing with her?' he hisses at me while she's eating. 'You've got to let them know she's here. I mean, is she adopted or what? She can't just take off like that. She's under age. We might be kidnapping, aiding and abetting – anything! She's got to go back. Back to the mill. That's where she belongs.'

'No chance,' I say.

'Now listen, Rachel . . .' (Here we go, he's doing his responsible older brother bit.) 'When children are up for adoption, the agencies concerned vet the prospective parents very, *very* thoroughly. You must be mistaken about this Silk guy. Come into the real world.'

'I know what I know!' I shout and Wally slinks under the table and leans against Sally's legs and she pats him and scowls at us.

'I know I'm right, Sam. And if I'm wrong, well . . . She needs us to take care of her. She can sleep in the little box-room. I can make up the bed. No need to stir yourself to do *anything*.'

'We can't just take her in, Rachel. You can't just charge into the situation like that.'

'*Oh yes I can!*' I hiss. 'Just listen to me for once, boss man. Go and look at her arms. And take it from me, she's in that state all over.'

He sighs his long-suffering-big-brother sigh, ambles

across the kitchen, glances at Sally's forearms, and turns chalk white.

He's straight back, nodding. 'All right, Rachel, yes, of course, she stays.'

She was staying anyway, Sam, but I'm glad we're in agreement.

Sally makes a brave attempt on the fry-up but at last she has to give up. She has eaten all the baked beans, but she doesn't like the burger and gives it to waiting Wally, who thinks it's Christmas. I suppose her stomach just hasn't been used to so much filling.

Sam is silent as he clears the table. He doesn't wash up much nowadays. When we knew Mum was ill we got a dishwasher to save time. Time for what?

Sally curls on the sofa looking at clothes and make-up in my magazine. She's tired and at about nine o'clock she falls asleep. Daft Sam puts on the rugby highlights at full volume and she wakes with a jolt. She sits up, blinking around, confused and fearful.

'Sally, it's all right. You're safe here with Sam and me,' I tell her.

'But it's a monster box, look!' she shrieks, pointing at the big men in stripes galumphing about on green.

'No, it's a television. Cameras take the pictures and we watch them.'

'Mr Silk says we must not look at that box! Or the

monsters inside will climb out and get us.' She's next to me now. I smile to myself. Some of my friends would love those stripy monsters to climb out of the telly and get *them*.

But Sally is trembling. 'Come on, let's leave the silly monsters,' I say loudly and Sam scowls at me as we go upstairs.

'Where's Daniel?' she says. 'I've never been without him. And he always reads to me. Then I can sleep.'

I know we have a big book of fairytales somewhere. I find it in a box in the cupboard, destined for a charity shop or jumble sale. It never got there. It must have known Sally was on her way. When I was at primary school I did shared reading with some infants. Sally must be quite a few years older. I honestly cannot tell. I'm sure she wouldn't under-stand teenage books. She has been brought up in such an odd place. What does the world look like through Sally's eyes?

'I want Rapunzel, please,' says Sally.

I'd forgotten the story – Rapunzel with her long golden hair, taken by a witch in payment for some fresh lettuce the girl's mother craved when she was pregnant! It's nasty really. The girl is shut up in the stone tower, gaoled by the horrid old witch, loved by the prince who climbs up that wonderful hair. Rescue? No chance. He just gets his eyes put out by thorns. I hadn't realised how horrible it was. He wanders in the desert, blind.

'I don't like this bit,' says Sally. 'Daniel used to miss it out.'

'What stories does he tell you, Sally?' I ask.

'Stories to stop me feeling the cold and the dark. *Goldilocks and the Three Bears* 'cos we eat a lot of porridge. And *Hansel and Gretel* 'cos I like the gingerbread house and the oven.'

'What about *Cinderella*? *Beauty and the Beast*? *Aladdin*?'

'Yes! All of them! He used to scare me, being the Beast, making shadows on the wall. And he makes stupid jokes, like, "You look nice, Sally. If I was a crow I would say *caw*! *Cor*!" '

'All men make stupid jokes, Sally,' I tell her, and she smiles and takes my hand and I think it would be nice to have a kind of sister.

Better than *him* downstairs, bawling at the rugby players on the television screen.

I just wish Daniel was here. I wonder where he's got to. He'd know what to do, wouldn't he?

No. How could he? Strong as he is, Daniel doesn't know what goes on in the world outside the mill. He doesn't know about our times and the way things work. But I fear that Sally may just give up without him.

When I say goodnight to Sally, she murmurs, 'Rachel! You haven't locked me in.'

*

I wake up suddenly, and know I'm not alone.

Someone is looking down into my face. She is beautiful.

I know her!

Her eyes are dark with those little flecks of gold. Sam has the same gold flecks in his eyes. Dad and I have grey eyes.

This is my mum as she really is, as she really was, maybe even before she had us. When she was happy with Dad. Her face is full and soft and pearly with love.

This is my real mum. I can see her now.

She cradles me in her smile. I lie here, half awake, held in her gaze, and loved.

I keep my eyes half open, my mind soft. I don't want her to go away.

I don't think about how or why or whether she's there or if she can really see me. I just feel love.

She stays for ages! Now I can do anything.

24

'I can't not just do nothing!'

I grab the phone book.

'Who are you ringing, Rachel?' calls Sam.

'Anyone who might help, Mr Nosey Parker. Childline, children's charities, NSPCC.'

'What are you going to say? It's only your word.'

He makes me so mad! 'I can't not just do nothing,' I snap.

'Do you want me to do the talking? At least it'll be grammatical!'

'No I *don't* want you to do the talking.'

The man and woman who stand on the doorstep terrify Sally.

'They'll tell Mr Silk I'm here,' she whispers, peeping at them round the curtain.

'No, they'll help us, I'm sure,' I console her.

Sam brings them in.

The woman says, 'Hello, I'm Jean.' She wears caring navy blue and cream Shetland. The man introduces himself as Bob Simpson. He's got horrible organiser trousers with lots of pockets.

'Come and help me get some tea, Sally,' says Sam.

While they are in the kitchen, I give Jean and Bob Simpson the few details I have. I've already mentioned the bruises on the phone.

'Of course we're very concerned, Rachel,' says Jean. 'Thank you for bringing this to our attention.' Her eyes don't thank me. They are suspicious. She says, 'We will have to do a lot of checking up. It's hard to think this could have happened in the way you describe. I take it you've not suffered yourself?'

'No.'

She makes me feel as if I'm going to look very silly. Know what? I don't care.

'Well, we can provide therapy or counselling from experts, if that's appropriate. It depends on our findings.'

She means, whether or not they believe me. She is all smiles and at ease, but her eyes take everything in. I try to nudge empty crisp packets under the sofa with my foot but they rustle. There's a smear of chocolate on the telly screen. Wally's hair has made a black cobweb by the sofa where he likes to lie. Oh well. Who cares?

'And you say Sally lived at a – a mill? Where?'

'Narrow Dale Mill. It's up in Derbyshire.'

'I know it! I took my own children there in August. For a day out. Then on to Paradise Park. But the staff are charming! We were shown round by the owner himself. Now, what was his name . . .'

'Mr Silk.' I can hardly say it.

'That's right. He does the tour in full costume, doesn't he? He looked so suave and he was so knowledgeable. He does a lot for charity, you know.'

'I'm sure he does.'

She looks at me for a long moment. 'And you think it was someone at this mill who caused your friend such distress?'

'It wasn't *someone*. It was him. It was Silk.'

'I find this all rather hard to believe, Rachel,' she says, her voice full with doubt. 'Those theme places are inspected from every angle for the safety of the children. The staff are rigorously checked. I'm sure . . . especially if children stay there. The officials look at the premises the children will use.'

'They see what they are shown, that's all! They don't see what's really there. They wouldn't want to see!'

'It can't be the same man. He's so well respected,' she says doubtfully.

I'm not going to let go of this one. I don't care how adult and well-meaning and official they are. I trust myself and what I think and feel.

I take a deep breath and try to sound reasonable. I say, 'Maybe there is more to him than meets the eye. Don't forget I was there for nearly a week. And Sally was there for years.'

'How long exactly?' she says sharply.

'I'm not sure.'

'We'll be able to trace the children's beginnings,' says the man. 'There will be records.'

Sam brings tea on a tray and Sally follows him. She ignores Jean and Bob and plants herself down a few inches from the television. She peers at the buttons on the remote control. Jean kneels down to face her.

'Can you remember a children's home, Sally?' she says.

Sally is trying to look round her to see what's coming on the screen. Suddenly the television is her friend. It will save her from these busybodies.

Jean tries again. 'What is your first memory? Before you were at the mill?'

Sally says impatiently, 'I was adopted. I was adopted from a dealer for a *lot* of money. I'm very expensive, expensive indeed!'

'Who did you play with when you were a little girl, Sally?'

'Daniel.'

'Where is Daniel now?'

'Dunno.' Sally wriggles round Jean to see the television.

'Do you go to school?'

'Mrs Silk teaches me. Needlework and numbers. I'm a good 'prentice girl. And Daniel taught me to read. I'm good,' she says.

'Mrs Silk? Who is she?'

'She's Mr Silk's missus, of course.'

'Does she cuddle you, Sally?'

'No! Spare the rod and spoil the child, that's the way!'

'Do you remember toys, my dear?'

'Yes. I had a wooden duck you pull along. But Daniel threw it in the pond. And some dolls.'

'A bicycle? A PlayStation?'

'No! Course not!' Sally's getting cross with the stupid questions.

On the television, a black man in a chef's hat is pulling faces and chopping up red and yellow peppers for a stir-fry. Sally wants to watch him because it's much more fun than listening to earnest Jean. Sally crawls fast right up to the screen.

Jean gives up and turns to me.

'You've introduced us to your brother,' she nods and smiles in his direction, 'but where are your parents?'

Uh-oh. Now we'll get the parental neglect bit.

'Dad is on a course this weekend. He's coming back tonight.'

'And your mother?'

Here we go again. It doesn't seem to get any easier. I can't say it to her. I don't have to.

'Our mother died earlier this year,' says Sam. 'She had a brain tumour.'

'Oh. I'm so sorry,' says Jean. She gives me a quizzical look. She comes on with the softy approach but she's not stupid. I bet she's thinking, well, she's lost her mother, so she's a bit loopy and resentful. Bit disturbed. Perhaps she sees things that aren't there.

She glances at Sally, now deeply involved with noodles and soy sauce, and whispers, 'I would guess that Sally has some learning difficulties. A girl with special needs . . . she may have fantasised, Rachel. Sometimes unhappiness makes people tell tales. Untruths. Because it brings them sympathy and attention. It becomes hard to get at the truth. You've acted only really on suspicion. And I'm glad you did. Many of our cases begin with suspicion only.'

'It's *not* suspicion only. When Sally had her bath last night I saw that she was covered with bruises! Seeing is believing!'

She turns for help to my sensible big brother.

'Have you seen these bruises, Sam? Do you believe it?'

'Of course I haven't seen them!' he cries. 'She would be mortified! I could see marks on her forearms and wrists. That was enough for me!'

'I have to look,' she says.

146

The men go into the kitchen. I switch the telly off and Sally cries, 'Rachel, I like that man!'

'Sally. Please can I show this lady how hungry you've been? How thin you are?'

'No!'

'If you let her see how thin you are, you can watch lots of telly again and I've got some chocolate biscuits. Hob Nobs. Kit Kat, Sally.'

I hate myself. I've let in the outside world and it's pushy and horrible. She's angry. She's backing towards the door.

'Please, Sally.'

'Mr Silk will punish Daniel if I show them myself. And Daniel – Daniel will – Daniel is so angry. He will be dangerous. Then he will get into big trouble.'

'Sally, we'll try to find Daniel so you can be together. And if anyone is hurting you, we'll stop them,' says Jean.

'But it was my fault,' says Sally as I ease up the T-shirt. 'I was bad you see. Ever so bad and stupid. That's why I got hit.'

I hear Jean's sharp intake of breath as she looks at Sally's wounds.

At last she smooths down Sally's T-shirt and turns to me. She says, 'I need to make some phone calls, Rachel.'

Perhaps I've misjudged Jean. Her eyes are full of tears.

25

I'll never cry for you, Mr Silk

I am here in the mill again.

I am always here, always.

I can hear talking. Someone is talking to Sally. It's my voice, I think.

I say, 'When I've rested, I'll run away again. I will come and find you. I promise. And then, Sally, we will find another life.'

'I don't think she can hear you, Daniel,' sneers the voice. 'Sally's not here. She's gone. And if you ever did escape, Daniel, who would believe you? Look at you!'

I spread my filthy, scratched hands. I know what he's saying is true.

Mr Silk stands quite still in front of me. It's as if he has grown up out of the floor.

'So she hasn't come back yet, Daniel? Do you think she ever will?'

There is a shake in his voice, which he tries to cover up.

'I have driven all over Derbyshire. I've been round towns and villages, hills and dales, and I can't find her. But there'll be a simple answer, Daniel. She's a simple girl.'

I say nothing.

'Who does Sally know, apart from you?'

I won't speak to him.

'Come on, Daniel, she must know someone. Think hard. A lot of things depend on it. Is there anyone she might know? Anyone she might have met? Someone she might go to?'

There's a window at the back of my mind letting in a glimmer of daylight. It's a small skylight, far away above me. That girl. Rachel. She had followed Sally. She must have talked to her. After that, it was as if Sally had some secret she kept from me. Or was I imagining it? Is it just because I like thinking of that girl, Rachel, with her shiny fall of hair and her quick look that knows me? I didn't think there would be a girl like that. Sally is the only girl I've known.

Rachel is different.

I mustn't tell Silk. I mustn't say a word.

'What about the visitors, Daniel? Could Sally have slipped away from you and met one . . . a boy, perhaps?'

Silk peers slyly at me to see my reaction.

'You wouldn't really like her to meet a boy, would you, Daniel? You like to be the only boy in her life, don't you? All right then . . . suppose she went hanging around where she wasn't supposed to go?'

Don't look at him. Don't say a word.

'Or she might have met up with one of those girls. Which one would it be, Daniel?'

He's playing cat and mouse again. I can play that game too. He'll pretend to lose interest until I think I may have freedom, and then –

'Let's talk about something different, Daniel. Mrs Silk and myself are carers. We have cared for you both for many years. Do you know where you were before that, Daniel?'

'No.'

There is excitement in his voice. I have learned over the years to dread that excitement.

'Let me give you some idea, Daniel. There are many stories about your parents. You could both be orphans. Let's see – your parents could be dead, killed in a car crash on the A6. They could be alcoholics. Heroin addicts. They could be in prison. For violent crimes, for murder. Or they might be nice middle-class people who – and I'm sorry to say this – who just didn't want you. So they turned you out. Literally.'

'Where did you find us?' It was out before I could stop myself. Don't ask anything of him. It puts you in his power.

'You were supplied to me through a middleman, Daniel. A dealer.'

'I remember the Dealer. He had a sickly smell.'

'That's as may be. He deals in such commodities as dispossessed orphans. He found you in a house on the south coast. Where was it now? The name of the town escapes me. Something-on-Sea . . .'

'Do you mean we were in a children's home?'

He gives a snickering laugh. 'That's not what I'd call it. I don't think anyone would give that place a licence. I paid a lot of money for you, Daniel. But I could always send you back there. With or without Sally.'

I couldn't bear life here without Sally, alone, in the dark!

'Tell me, Daniel, who did she make friends with? I won't be cross. It's nice for Sally to have friends, isn't it? Otherwise she only knows you in the whole wide world, and that's putting all her eggs in one basket, isn't it?'

If Sally has got away, then better she takes her chance than comes back here with him. She has no future. So what if I am sent back to this home? I couldn't bear Sally suffering again. She's gone to find that Rachel, hasn't she? Pretty, knowing Rachel with the long legs. Will she look after Sally or send her back? Can we trust her? What are people really like?

Silk places long fingers on his chin, in speculation.

'Do you know, my dear wife thinks it may be a particular one of those girls! It seems she saw Sally with a gold pen. She took it from her and gave it back to me. It was initialled, R.W. Perhaps it was a gift? Sally said she found it. Do you believe that? Eh, Daniel?'

He reaches out and touches my ear. I tense and wait. I see his long white neck. It has strings in it, tightened up to the surface. I could fit my hands round that neck and squeeze.

He twists my ear. It hurts, it really hurts, *but I'll never cry for you, Mr Silk.*

'Of course, I have all their addresses,' he says.

Again he twists as if he is trying to snap the dead bloom from a flower.

Pain. I bite my lip hard and taste blood.

'So really, it doesn't matter what you say, Daniel, or what you don't say. I can always pay them a visit to see if they've heard anything of our dear girl. I can keep watch on their houses. Sally should be back here. This is her home. This is where she will end her days.' He pushes me away from him, hard, against the wall.

The door opens and closes.

My back hurts and I want to be sick. I stare at the floor and see a bloodstain spreading on the stone. In my head I turn it into Silk's face, his smile and his long nose and his dead eyes. And then I spit, hard. My aim is true.

The mill room is so cold. I often think we may die in our sleep, Sally and I. We slow down and almost stop. That would be a peaceful escape.

I am calm now and I know what I must do.

I find my wooden box of marbles and play a game carefully on the stone floor. It's uneven for marbles, it always has been, but I know its slopes and dips and how to play the best.

I take a blanket to put round my shoulders for a cloak. Much of the snow has melted but the winter still has its cold grip.

I ease myself up. Drag myself over to the window. I ache, my body has jagged flame running through it.

There's no little bird today. I try to see myself down by the millpond, try to catch my reflection. In the jet water my pale jelly face quivers, my mouth a dumb O. I am a wild-haired brown-skinned boy, as if I have lived out by a smoking fire in the woods. Down in the water I am already a ghost.

I know it's all still out there, the mill sheer as a cliff, the glinting river, the still pond and the little road out to the rest of the world, the white pigs rooting in their field.

The black car sits in the yard. Silk is in the office, I'm sure, going through the list of summer children, looking at their addresses. And then he'll decide where to search for Sally.

I talk to Sally in my head: *Fear of Silk makes you obedient. Fear of Silk fills me with rage. I don't care now what happens. All I want is for you to be safe from him for ever. There is no sense in the world while he can hurt you again and again. I do not want to live in that kind of world.*

It seems to me that I have heard angry water all my life. Now it wells up in me, a rage ready to spill over. In the far distances of the earth the river pounds through the rock, restless and muddied, before it reaches the mill and is stilled in the pond.

Now that the snow has melted the waters are deep. I feel their power like a charge.

I can wait. A little longer makes no difference after all these years.

I drift in and out of sleep. I dream-walk through a street of tall houses with pointed, sloping roofs and gables. They are blood red and close under a starless sky.

In the dream I know where I am, I know the red city, but I can't find my way out. There are no street signs, no gaps between the buildings and the windows are in darkness. No people, no cars, but there are tall trees with leaves that rustle in the breeze. The leaves begin to swirl in the street and the wind grows stronger and stronger so that I can hardly stand up! I turn to see the wind coming down the street towards me, or is it water? The torrent of water! I wake up, sick with fear.

For a dizzy moment I believe I'm still in the dark red city. Then I smell wax.

The candle has burned out.

'Sally?' I call. The dream wind was the downstairs door opening and the air rushing up the spiral staircase. I hear quick steps on the stairs. They are not Silk's steps! They pause outside my door. The bolts are pulled back slowly, not easily.

154

It's his wife. She carries a tray. There are eggs with middles like big yellow eyes, a stack of toast and a mug of tea. She puts it down on the table.

'Survival rations, Danny,' she says, trying to put brightness into her voice.

'Come on, now. The Master has gone out. You had better eat to build up your strength.'

I eat. I wolf down that food. I don't care that she is watching me so eagerly.

'When will Sally be back?' she asks. 'I miss seeing her. Such beautiful hair. I would have liked a daughter.' For a moment I think she's going to cry.

'Where is she, Daniel?'

'How should I know?'

She says, 'The Master misses her, you know. He's *so* fond of her.' Her voice is peevish as a little old hinge.

I don't want to look at her but I can smell her; a mix of perfume and acid sweat.

The querulous voice witters on. 'She means so much to him. And to you, Danny, I can tell. You're lost without her, aren't you?'

I stare at the yellow eggy smears on my plate, wipe them round with my finger.

She puts her hand on my shoulder.

'You are sure she left *with* you, aren't you, Danny?'

I pause. I realise that she is terrified. She thinks Sally may

155

still be here somewhere. She thinks he may –

'Where could she be, Daniel? We ought to find her. She has a problem, you know, with bleeds in her head. She had one when she was a baby. They don't know why. Some weakness in her veins. That is why her eye is damaged. If things get bad, she might have another one. It's a bit like the sluice gates when the river is full. It's already damaged her brain. Another bleed could kill her.'

I lick egg off my fingers and squeeze my eyes tight shut.

'Come on, Daniel,' she wheedles. 'Think of the dreadful things that could happen to her.'

I already have. I never stop thinking of dreadful things. How could I think of nice things?

'It's cold and she'll starve and – Daniel, think of the men out there. Think what they might do to her. She's an innocent. She's bewildered and confused; she needs to come back here with you. Where could she be? Tell me, and I'll see what I can do,' she coaxes.

'I don't know where she is!' I shout. 'And why don't you think about your husband! Think what he might do to Sally? Think how he hurts her, Mrs Silk!'

She can't speak. She fusses around, picking up the candle stubs, tidying Sally's empty bed, rearranging the little dolls on the pillow all over again.

Then she warns, 'The Master will get angry. He – he's got a temper, you know. If he finds her he'll punish her. Let me find her first, Daniel. I know you depend on Sally. You like girls, don't you? What about that one last week?' She gives my shoulder a little squeeze.

'What girl last week?'

'That girl Rachel. The pretty one with the dark hair who stayed for the holiday week. Don't tell me you didn't spy on her, Daniel.'

I turn my head fast and sink my teeth into her fat hand.

She shrieks and steps back from me.

'You'll be sorry you didn't help me!' she screams. 'It'll be worse with him, you'll see!'

She sucks the wound of her bitten hand and I turn on her, shouting, 'Why didn't you stop him, you foolish woman? Why did you never protect us?'

Tears trickle down her cheeks.

She whispers, 'I *did*.'

Somehow she finds her way to the door and leaves me to pain. And darkness.

26

On the roof of the world

Sam says, 'My sister's not right very often, Jean.'

I'm ready to snap off his head when he follows with, 'But this time she may be right. This time we have to think about Sally, don't we, and if she wants to go with you, then she must.'

'It's quite inappropriate,' insists Jean, 'quite out of order for you girls to come with us.'

Sally hears that, freezes and turns into someone else. She turns into a demon, her head aflame. She picks up our old piano stool, whirls it above her head and hurls it at Jean. Jean ducks, Bob side-steps and the stool lands on the sofa.

Wally tries to dig himself into the corner of the room.

Sam folds his arms, ever cool, ever the observer and I just want to laugh. I'm not shocked by Sally's rage. It fills me with a sort of energy.

'I'm not staying here!' she roars. 'I'm coming with you,

I'm coming to find Danny.' She begins to kick the armchair, a slow, solid rhythm. Then she stops, thinking. She turns to Jean and says craftily, 'Daniel won't come anywhere near you if I'm not there.'

Silence.

Sam says, 'I could follow in my car and bring Sally.'

'And me too!' I cry. 'She wouldn't come without me!'

Jean studies each of us in turn. I think she realises she'll get nowhere unless she gives in. Sally is stubborn. I suppose I had a vague picture of her as pathetic, because of what's happened to her. Now I see that she can be hard as a rock.

Jean still tries, not very hard: 'But it will be such a shock to re-visit the mill, Sally,' she says. 'And you may see Mr Silk. It will possibly be traumatic.'

'Trow what?' shouts Sally. 'Who cares! I'm going to get Daniel! I'm going up the stairs to the room and I'll find him!' She lowers her voice as if she is explaining something unquestionable to a little child. 'You see, Daniel is always there.'

Jean sighs in defeat.

We have to hang around for what seems ages while Jean and Bob make phone calls. Sally doesn't mind. She eats apples and crisps and watches television. Wally slinks out from his corner and sits drooling by her. She feeds him crisps. I know Sam wants to stop her. He doesn't agree with people's titbits for dogs.

I just want to get on with it. Unlike Sally, I don't believe Daniel will be anywhere near the mill. I fear for him. I fear for both of them.

At last the police turn up. Wally doesn't like the look of the strange men, even though they're not in funny hats, and he goes mad, doing Hound of the Baskervilles noises. The police dither and look uncomfortable, but Jean seems sure of what she's doing.

She goes with them to a station 'for procedures'. We follow on after a while in Sam's car. It seems years since my visit to the mill, that bright autumn day. How long ago was it? A few weeks? I remember shoals of golden leaves scudding down the street as we waited for the horse and cart.

The world has changed since then.

'Shall we stop on the grass for a minute?' suggests Sam, pulling in anyway. Sometimes my brother isn't as thick as I think. We are on the B road high on the ridge before the little road snakes down into Narrow Dale, on a verge by a stone wall.

'Let's get out and take some air,' says Sam. 'It'll do us all good.'

The wind buffets us towards a gate. We grip it, eyes streaming, bodies chilled.

Sheep look in our direction, bleat and then flounder away down the slope.

'We're kings and queens!' shouts Sally.

For we are on the roof of the world! Before us stretch hills and headlands, rearing up to the blue sky. They jostle each other for space. It is an ancient, restless landscape, like a sea of rock with pools of velvet green cropped close by sheep. Somewhere out in that wild earth is Narrow Dale, with its gleam of water. Narrow Dale is just a lesion, hidden away from the world. And in its small, secret fold is the mill. You could easily overlook it.

'The mill is down there, Sally,' I tell her. 'When you're out here with all this earth and sky you can't believe it, can you?'

'Daniel is down there,' she says, but her voice falters.

27

Suppose I'm wrong?

So here we are.

I don't really know what I've got myself into. I mean, if they arrest Mr Silk, will I have to give evidence, or what? Do I have to swear on the Bible? How will I speak in a court? How will I say the right thing? Will I remember?

Dad will have to come with me. I want him to.

What about Sally, will she have to be cross-examined? Will she have to show her cuts and bruises to hundreds of doctors and lawyers and police and feel dreadfully embarrassed?

They'll have faded by then, surely?

All these questions and thoughts buffet round my head. Suddenly the mill is there again.

'The mill is very big,' whispers Sally. I realise that she's never approached it by road before, not since she was a young child anyway. She puts her hand in mine. It's cold and so I give it a gentle squeeze.

'Our window is up there!' she cries.

I don't answer her because the little window is in darkness. The flame has gone out. We've left it too long.

'We should wait in the car,' says Sam, switching off the engine. We're in the courtyard. So is an unmarked car, but the men peering in through the windows wear blue shirts.

'Mr Silk lives in the house at the end,' says Sally and her voice is shaking.

There's no one here after all. They've gone. The mill is empty, they've had time to go.

A small sound. A figure stands framed in the doorway.

I realise with horror that now I know his face so well! A frown, a doubt flits across it. Not fear, just a small fracture in his confidence. He hesitates. And then, a wide smile. How cool and calm he looks. He walks towards Bob Simpson, official, but welcoming, his hand held out. Sam winds down the window but we can't hear what's being said.

'They'll ask him to go down the nick, I should think,' says Sam. 'To have a talk with them. He doesn't look bothered, does he?'

'He wouldn't,' I say. 'He's such an actor.'

The Master of the Mill is smiling and waving his graceful hands. He is the charming host welcoming his visitors.

Sally is standing up in the car, craning her neck to look, but not at Silk. She covers her bad eye but she still can't see properly. She says, 'I can't see the room from here. I can't see the candle in the window. Will they find Daniel now?'

She opens the door to look out.

'They'll have a big search with lots of police and people to help, I'm sure.'

I turn back to watch Silk and Bob. Soon Mr Silk is striding across the yard back to his door. 'He'll be going to get a coat or something,' says Sam.

I concentrate on opening a packet of sweets, my favourite squidgy green mints. I'm shaking with terror in spite of myself! Suppose I'm wrong and things *are* what they seem? What a fool I'll look, what trouble I'll get into and Miss Benson will be proved right after all. She'll never shut up about it, she'll tell everyone, she'll. . . . I scrabble and take out the first mint – paper off, into my mouth – then start edging out the next mint from the silver paper for Sally.

She's not next to me. She's gone.

She must have darted round the millpond. I follow her, with thoughts tumbling in my head. She's gone to see if he's in their room. She's trying to escape us all.

And then I hear her name: *Sally*! *SALLY*! cried out across the dale, echoing back from the high stone walls of the mill.

Daniel is running down the dale from the trees, running to meet her.

They are two angels in an old oil painting; the dark angel and the angel of light with the brightness round her head.

'Sally! Sally!' he shouts. 'Look out!'

Because after her purrs the black car, along the narrow edge of the pond.

Mr Silk has been getting his keys, getting into his car, getting Sally.

He's driving right up against the millpond. He's going to force her into the pond, isn't he?

The car stops at last, the wheel hanging over the muddy bank. Then out of the passenger door slides that figure. I'm watching a film. He's moving so slowly, but he'll catch her, he will!

Daniel is pounding along the bank.

Who will reach her first? Who –?

Silk lopes across the mud towards Sally, his long arms outstretched, the hands reaching out for her, but just as he reaches her, he slips.

He's gone. Silence.

28

Follow your heart

Daniel and Sally stand near each other, quite still.

Sally puts her arms behind her back and locks her hands together tightly.

I remember, now. I can hear Mr Silk's laughing voice: 'Water is not my element!'

He can't swim.

His head crowns in the water, his hair drenched against his skull, white, his mouth gasping and grinning, his arm reaches out towards them.

Daniel and Sally look at each other.

Then Daniel glances away. He turns towards me; our eyes meet and what we both know passes between us.

Someone shouts, 'DON'T!'

Daniel crouches, stretches one arm out over the bank towards the drowning man, the other arm in front of Sally to stop her falling. Slowly she brings her arms round to the front and she too holds out her hand.

I've almost reached them. Silk's eyes make me think of peeled boiled eggs, all grey and white; they're horrible! He snatches at Daniel's hand and grasps it. Then Sally's.

For a split second he holds both their hands, then he pulls, hard.

He's pulling them in. He's going to drown them in that deep dark water, I can see it twisted on his face! He hates them. He loves them too. He's going to take them with him.

And then there's not just Sally and Daniel, there's me and Sam too, holding on to them and dragging Silk out of the millpond. It's as if he's stuck in quicksand. He's soaking and slow. A sea god heavy with loathing. He doesn't want to be saved. Not by them, not by anyone, because they see him for what he is.

There are footsteps running up behind us.

He's out. They're dragging him away and he's shouting so I cover up my ears. I don't have to hear him. I can't look at him. I don't want to see his vengeful face as he's taken away or I'll never forget it. I won't anyway.

The water settles and smooths over the tumult. A little bird slips into the pond and begins its voyage round and round.

Someone else is near us, a dumpy figure, looking up at Jean. Her brown hair is not in its tight little bun. It falls softly round her shoulders. She looks young with it like that.

'I tried to stop him, you know,' says Mrs Silk so earnestly. 'But he had such a thing about the past.' She notices me. 'Oh, Rachel,' she cries. 'I'm glad Sally is with you.'

Her eyes follow her husband. They fill with tears. She says, 'I must go with him. He needs me.'

I realise that Silk is her whole life. Perhaps he *will* need her now.

Sally and Daniel stand near each other, arms hanging loosely by their sides. They're not talking. I don't know if they'll ever be able to speak again.

Their faces are unguarded and soft.

How young they look, especially Sally.

Jean is here saying brightly, 'Sally and Daniel won't move far away, Rachel. We have a policy of keeping children in the same area, near people they know.'

She sees the expression on my face and says hastily, 'I don't mean near the mill, dear. I mean perhaps in Nottingham or Derby. It would be good for her to feel ties with you and Sam. I think you have a strong bond with Sally.'

And I'd like a strong bond with her friend too, but of course I don't tell Jean.

I turn away and hurry to them. They look more like themselves again now.

Daniel looks straight at me. I meet those dark, fathomless eyes and my heart gives a little pang. He's dangerous.

'Rachel,' he says. 'You kept her safe. Thank you.'

He looks at me as if it is the first time he's seen me.

Sally says, 'Daniel, you look all bleeding and horrible.'

'Do I, Sally?' he scowls.

She smiles up at him, all clean and brushed and in new clothes. In Daniel's face I see irritation, familiarity, resentment, and the need to protect her. A bit like Sam's need to protect me, and sometimes I don't want that because I want to be independent. But I quite like knowing I can rely on Sam . . . Big brothers have their uses. And I think suddenly of my dad, and curry.

A smile spreads slowly across Daniel's face. He smiles down at Sally, and then looks across at me. In his face I see humour and affection flowing over the irritation and worry.

I've seen these feelings before somewhere, sometimes all these things at once. It's not any one of them, it's all of them, shifting and shining together. It's love. That simple, complicated crazy feeling you can have for all kinds of people. The feeling that makes everything possible.

And if you've been loved once, really loved, you can do anything. You can throw away your fear and trust your own mind and just be yourself.

Someone has already told me all about this. Wasn't I lucky! I didn't want to hear it then. But now, Mum, I know you're right.